Earthly Delights and Other Apocalypses

Earthly Delights
and Other Apocalypses

Winner of the 2018 Press 53 Award for Short Fiction

Jen Julian

Press 53
Winston-Salem

Press 53, LLC
PO Box 30314
Winston-Salem, NC 27130

First Edition

Cover design by Claire V. Foxx & Kevin Morgan Watson

Cover art, "The Girl and the Forest," Copyright © 2017
by Alekseyliss, licensed through iStockPhoto.

Author photo by Heather Renee Brand

Library of Congress Control Number
2018955647

Printed on acid-free paper
ISBN 978-1-941209-91-2 (paperback)
ISBN 978-1-941209-92-9 (hardcover)

to my parents, Brenda and Phil,
who have been there since the beginning

The author thanks the editors of the following publications for first publishing these stories:

Beecher's Magazine: "One for Sorrow, Two for Joy" (2017)

Cleaver Magazine: "We Are Meant for Greater Things" (2015)

Greensboro Review: "Little Ones Weary" (2016)

New Delta Review: "Stereograms" (2013)

New South: "Castle Links Creek" (2015)

Tahoma Literary Review: "Bone Men" (2015)

TriQuarterly: "Attachment" (2018)

Contents

Bone Men   1

Keepers   15

One for Sorrow, Two for Joy   33

Stereograms   43

Castle Links Creek   63

We Are Meant for Greater Things   75

Attachment   83

Earthly Delights   89

I'm Here, I'm Listening   107

Little Ones Weary   145

Author biography   159

Bone Men

Some years after her mother left them, her father was called to Cornell to lecture on recent fossil finds in southern Germany. On the train, they sat facing each other and barely spoke, and she realized, as sunlight flickered in through the window of the dining car, that he had gone dry from the inside out. It was as if his whole body had become filled with air, as if some internal current of gray breeze was the sole thing that kept him standing.

They changed trains in Chicago, and the long bouts of silence had left her body a taut string of anxiety and excitement. She had never been in a city so large. How strange that it seemed cripplingly claustrophobic despite its size. A recent rain had left the train station damp with the fog-thick smell of garbage and manure. Manure—that was what one of her father's colleagues had once told her about cities—you would not believe the manure in those places, and as she and her father rode their new train eastward, she saw great piles of it on the outskirts of the city, tall enough to cover a man to the crown of his head. She saw where the horses themselves had been dumped, worked to death, their stark-ribbed hides marred with scars from the harnesses. The smell of rot filled the train.

"That's horrible," she said, and when her father didn't respond, she said it again. "My God, that's horrible."

Her father kept his eyes on his papers and lecture notes. The horse graveyard had devolved into bones, long yellow grass growing between sun-bleached ribs.

"Do you see that?" she asked.

Her father lifted his head, perhaps sensing the urgency in her voice. He pushed his reading glasses onto his forehead and looked out the window, kept looking until the graveyard had fallen away in place of farmland.

"It is horrible," her father said. "But men need to get to wherever they're going."

And there it was, just like that: her resentment. It always reminded her of the lionfish spines her father had once brought from Venice Beach, hollow, venomous flutes capable of taking down a beast as large as a manta ray. No matter how much she swelled with love and respect for her father, it took just these small moments, these brief stabs, to make her hate him.

"I don't see why the concerns of men are so much more important than the concerns of horses," she said.

Her father cleared his throat and returned to what he'd been reading.

It was clear he didn't even want to be here, on this train, on the way to Ithaca; he'd been reduced to doing his job out of rote. One lecture. Another. Research. Revise. Part of her blamed her mother, the woman who had abandoned the two of them to a melancholy state and a decrepit patch of farmland. But at the same time, she consented it was possible that her father was getting older, and that all men were like this when they got older. The battlefields on which they had skirmished became irrelevant. When they finally arrived at Cornell, she hoped in vain that his reception would at least partly mirror the competitive conferences in Kansas, when the war for government funding was at its height between her father and a hotheaded rival, who'd since drunk himself to death. Now, there was a careless humor regarding his lectures, a sense that the field of paleontology had become little more than a contest to see who could put together a jigsaw puzzle the fastest. When it came to light that the brontosaurus was not even real, that the species was a misassembled version of something that had already been discovered, it cemented an atmosphere of embarrassment over her father's area of study, like the achy, foul-tasting haze the morning after a wild party.

(Not that she knew anything about wild parties.)

Even professors outside of the field—the chemists, the mathematicians, the engineers—weighed in with smug opinions (they were the smuggest, weren't they, engineers). These paleo-men, how did they know what went together? They didn't really; it was all guesswork. It wasn't even really *science* because there was no way to know if you were right when you worked with materials millions of years old. In fact, it took some crackerjack in England twenty years to figure out that he'd had the wrong skull on the wrong animal—a riotous joke, one of many jokes. This was what became of men who obsessed over the past, who kept themselves buried in dead fragments of bone and rock—diggers, dirt men, *old* men.

She worked hard to fend off this environment of disdain. If only her father weren't so serious, she thought. If he only just laughed with the others, he could slough off their jokes. Instead, he absorbed them the way dust absorbs sound, and they dried him out further.

The Cornell lecture was in three parts. He gave the first that evening, just four hours after getting off the train. A disaster. Everyone in the auditorium could tell he was exhausted, his voice staggering its way, just barely, past the middle rows. Not that this mattered much; the audience wouldn't be large enough to play a decent game of baseball. His lectern had a nail loose, and so it wobbled, his papers sliding off onto the stage, but he didn't pick them up, just kept going, the notes written on the back of his eyeballs like lantern slides. She watched from the front row, aware of the eyes burning into the back of her head. She was the only woman in the room. At one point, determined not to shrink or wither, she turned to look at the young men behind her: a collective of fresh-faced scholars with the slicked-back style of East Coast boys. She wanted to look defensive, a woman staunch in her admiration of the man on stage, but she had never had to play this role before, and she felt she did it poorly, more petulant child than strong daughter. Did they know she was his daughter? Should she tell them?

Afterward, when they had settled in at the house of an old colleague, her father took an afternoon rest, and she laid herself down like she was tired. Really, she was too restless to sleep. She thought about horses, scarred flesh and foaming mouths, worked to death. Through the open windows of the colonial house, she heard the raucous barks of male laughter on the sidewalks, their crude language made cruder with the heat of late May. Without a word to anyone else, she was up and outside, the sound of life goading her on.

It impressed her, this sluggish heat, how the sunlight poured on the ground like syrup. She was used to the heat of the plains, which would dry out your mouth and nostrils overnight, but here the heat weighed you down and clung to your skin. She let herself sweat, made her way in a wide circle around the bell tower, and everywhere she saw students, upright pinnacles of youth and enthusiasm. There was something canine about them, their teeth flashing with ferocious smiles, eyes on fire, and she straightened her spine in the light of their faces. It was unusual, pleasurable maybe, feeling inspected, feeling looked at, but she neither encouraged nor discouraged it, choosing to occupy an empty bench at the edge of the quad to demonstrate her indifference. She was not there five minutes when a young man approached her.

"Have I seen you?" he asked.

She looked up at him. He had an amiable expression, somewhat manic, like one easily distracted. He was fair-headed, tanned and athletic, a big round sailor's jaw.

"I was there at the lecture this morning," she said.

He laughed. "Oh, the presentation."

"He's my father. Did you know he was my father?"

The young man's smile flickered with embarrassment, as if she had stopped him from saying what he would say next.

"It was a fine lecture," he said.

"It was bunkum," she said.

"It—all right, it wasn't *my* interest personally, I'll admit. And the boys and I agreed he did seem like he'd been hitting the drink the night before."

"He's just tired," she said. "That's all."

He reached into his back pocket and pulled out a tin of Turkish cigarettes. "One from the hope chest?"

She smiled. A trickle of sweat ran down the side of her face.

"It's true what they say about university boys, isn't it," she said.

The young man stared at her, his eyebrows arched, the manic smile lingering on his handsome face. "We'd be disappointed if you thought otherwise."

His name was Tom. He was an engineering student at Cornell, but his secret passion was chemistry. He carried the periodic table around in his pocket like a love letter, so worn that the paper had become soft and pliable. When he placed it into her hand, she felt the warmth from where it had been hiding.

The second lecture went better, which pleased and surprised her. She'd worried she was being selfish or improper when she accepted Tom's offer to sit with him toward the back of the auditorium. Firstly, she had not asked for her father's permission to do this, and secondly, she was anxious that he would notice her absence in the first row, that he would think she had betrayed him. But his focus seemed much clearer than it had the day before, and if he realized she had changed her seat, it did not affect his performance.

"He did used to be much statelier," she whispered to Tom as the lecture carried on. Her father revealed his diagrams of hollowed-out bird bones, his recreation of the feathered Archaeopteryx. "See, he drew that. He taught me how when I was a little girl."

Tom leaned toward her. "If I asked you, would you draw me?"

"Why would you ask me that? Stop being foolish and pay attention."

Behind them, someone overheard their whispered conversation and snorted with laughter. Someone else hissed through his teeth to quiet him.

Afterward, when her father had finished talking to the students and professors who had gathered to ask him questions, she introduced Tom as a friend she'd met. Her father barely reacted, his expression vague. When she leaned in to kiss his cheek, she caught an earthy smell and saw that odd, clay-like fractures had formed around his eyes.

"This is wearing you out," she said.

"Nothing I can't manage," he told her. "Just one more and then we'll head home. I promise."

His words, she realized, sounded as empty as the house that waited for them. This concerned her, but she still let Tom lead her out of the auditorium, leaving her father behind.

Tom said he wanted to show her the falls, because she couldn't come to Ithaca and not see the falls; that'd be a travesty. When they arrived, several young men were swimming in the shallows among the rocks, and she watched them, hypnotized, their dorsal muscles tightening like tiny white wings. They shouted as they belly-flopped into the pool, hooting about how cold it was, the thick heat of the air mingling with the shock of the water against their skin. When they saw Tom, they called for him to remove his clothes and dive in.

"I can't swim," she said quietly.

Tom didn't answer. She felt his breath on the back of her neck. He took her wrist and pulled her into the shadows of the trees.

When he laid her down under a cypress, she could feel his heart thumping heavily against her own. He rubbed a piece of her hair with his thumb and forefinger, staring her down as if she had appeared in front of him by magic. "Where in the world did you come from?" he asked.

"Kansas," she said.

When he broke her hymen, the pain was brief and strange, accompanied by a weird heat that rippled through her fingers and toes. She wasn't sure if she could call it pleasure, painful as it was, but it fascinated her, the way all new sensations fascinated her: the burn of a hot pepper on the tongue, the itch of a scab healing. Afterward, she lay puzzled, feeling languid, though not in any way distressed. By contrast, Tom had not yet spent his nervous energy. He stood up, still naked, and began doing pull-ups on an overhanging cypress branch. She watched him and eventually forced herself to say something.

"Do you ever worry about the horses?" she asked.

Tom grunted between pull-ups. The branch bounced with his weight. "Horses?"

"I worry about the horses," she said. "The ones in Chicago. In all cities, really. They get worked until they fall over dead in their harnesses. Whatever you believe, whether you think God exists or not—I know a lot of you educated men don't—you can't think it's good for human beings to treat living things that way." When Tom didn't reply, she lowered her eyes, picked at the skin around her fingers. "I worry about the horses more than I worry about my father. I guess that's wrong, isn't it."

Tom was thoughtful, his chin resting on his knuckles. "Poor things," he said, and it wasn't clear if he was talking about just the horses, or the horses and her father both. He let himself drop, his socked feet landing heavy on the leafy ground. "You shouldn't worry so much. In a few years, the horse will be an obsolete problem. The combustion engine is the future. My father owns a rubber factory in Dayton, Ohio. Tires. 'Where the road meets innovation.'"

She glanced up at him, her eyes resting briefly on his groin before traveling to meet his face. She felt shy about his nudity. "You're talking about autocars. But who can afford them? Who would want to? You can't even take them up a hill without them rolling down again backwards."

"That'll change," Tom said, undeterred. "Forward, Kansas. Forward always."

She mulled over this phrase for a moment, then receded into the shade of the cypress tree to clean the blood off her thighs. A deep, prehistoric part of her had caught fire for the first time, but she also felt a deadly sensation of shame creeping through her consciousness. She had become the slut her mother had told her about in stories, not that she put much stock in things her mother had told her nowadays. Had she thought even once to say no to Tom? No. His excitement and confidence had mesmerized her, still clearly in the earliest stages of its development, deceptively immature. She guessed this accounted for their attraction. They were both half-castes: no longer adolescents, not quite adults. There were four among them: man, woman, and the shades of two utopic children.

Once they had dressed, he walked her back to where she was staying, back to where her father napped over the notes of his final lecture.

Tom stood on the lawn and kissed her forehead.

"That was fun," he said. "We had a good time."

"We did," she said.

"Ever since I saw you in the auditorium yesterday, I thought, 'That girl's sweet. I want to show her around.' Tomorrow afternoon, I can take you over to the chem lab. This roommate of mine, he's put together this lulu of an apparatus that synthesizes ammonia."

"I'm leaving tomorrow," she told him, and saying the words aloud made her realize how relieved she was. She could take her exhausted father home to Kansas. She could rest knowing that Tom would be frozen in her mind, an imprint that she could take out to examine whenever she liked. Tom seemed stunned that she would turn him down so easily, would be so flippant about her departure, and this accentuated her shame. But he had all but admitted he was an aspiring rake, and in this case, maybe it was better to be a slut than a fool.

That night, as she washed her face and prepared for bed, she overheard the housekeeper complaining to herself about a trail of dirt in the foyer. She worried it was *she* who'd tracked it in, a mark of indiscretion that had followed her all the way from the cypress tree, but when she checked, her boots and dress were clean. She found more dirt—little bits of pale, dusty fragments—streaking the upstairs hall, and she followed it into the room where her father was staying. He sat at the desk, his books and journals splayed out in front of him.

"Did *you* make this mess?" she asked. "If you brought in samples for everyone to see tomorrow, you'll want to check on them. They may have fallen apart."

Her father turned his whole body to face her. He seemed more fractured than ever. His dark hair—she remembered being able to grip whole fistfuls between her fingers as a child—was little more than a few wiry wisps.

"Come sit down here," he told her.

She felt a guilty stitch of pain between her legs as she sat on the foot of his bed. Her father, with great effort, came over and sat next to her.

"The young man who's been escorting you around," he said. "He's quite vivacious."

"He's all right," she said, flicking her hand. "He's a bit tiring. I'll be happy to head home."

"We were all like that, so filled with energy," he said. "When you want to know things and you feel as if the world was made for you, it's like there's fire in your veins. I don't have much fire anymore. This slow death, it drove off your mother, and the same is happening with you."

"My mother?" she said. They stared at one another in silence, and she realized that something in her father had become dire, and she had been unable or unwilling to see it. "What does my mother have to do with any of this, with fire in the veins or otherwise? What do *I* have to do with it?"

"You don't understand what it's like," he said, "to feel like you've failed your child."

"Is it about your research?"

He opened his cracked mouth and closed it, his eyes fearful at the very mention of his work, and she realized bringing it up had been a mistake. Possibly, he had convinced himself she hadn't noticed the change in the collegial atmosphere, his relegation to that of a lesser scholar.

"I don't care what other people think about your research," she said desperately. "You're my *father*. You're *brilliant*."

He took a breath, which was the sound of gravel crunching underfoot. "I wish I could leave you with more."

She felt her chest splitting for him, for all the times she'd sat in his office while he worked or sketched or read aloud, Darwin or Lamarck, and she remembered emerging from these long sessions to find concern, or perhaps even envy, entrenched in her mother's face. She learned to be afraid of it, this face, marked with so many lines of disappointment. She recalled all the times she'd asked her mother, sitting blankly at the parlor window, what she was doing there, and she had answered back, always the same: "Nothing."

Now, with her father sitting next to her, she could sense what overwhelming powerlessness one could feel when afflicted with such a word. She needed to hear it, if only to confirm its brute force.

"Tell me what I can do for you," she said to him.

He told her: "Nothing."

"Then I will *do* nothing," she said.

As she stood, he reached for her arm, his fingertips like sandpaper. "Please don't be angry."

"I'll be how I want. Keep your fossils. Let them drain you dry. I don't care."

With that, she abandoned the conversation before anything else was said.

Late that night, as she willed herself to sleep, she prayed her father would realize that her fury was out of love, even though she knew she had hurt him. How betrayed he would feel to know that she had sneaked off to the falls and under a cypress tree with Tom, the engineer, the chemist, her legs wrapped around the body of her father's rival. She felt also that she'd betrayed him by being born a woman, so that now, in his old age, he had to watch her spirit steadily align with her mother's. There was nothing she could do about this. It seemed inevitable.

The next day, the afternoon of her father's third lecture, she saw Tom outside the auditorium, waiting for her. Four of his friends, spry, blond athletic types like himself, watched on with eager faces, but Tom sent them all away with a wave of his stocky hand. He transformed when she approached, switching on his manic smile, which flustered her. She wanted his gentlemanly enthusiasm to be a pretext so that she wouldn't have to worry about him. This young man had seduced women before; she had not been so naïve and pitiful under the cypress tree to have failed to realize that. And yet he was as dogged now as yesterday, pleased with her and with himself.

"Hello, Kansas," he said, holding up his arm. "May I take you inside?"

"Fine," she said. "But you sit in the front with me this time."

He agreed. They made their way up to the front and settled in.

"Did I tell you I write poetry?" he asked breathlessly. "I wrote a sonnet about you at four this morning."

"Your time would have been better spent sleeping," she told him.

He laughed, and his laughter rose above the general chatter of the auditorium. She quieted him when her father came out on the stage.

It went better, his best yet. He presented his materials with a solid voice, bright gestures, as if their talk the previous evening had regenerated some of his enthusiasm. She felt her pride in him rekindle as she observed and listened. Raptor, Archaeopteryx, emu—the ancestral line of the dinosaur. The audience, if not genuinely impressed, was silent, respectful of her father's clarity.

But as she watched, he began to shed dust.

She felt Tom's thumb massaging her wrist, working its way up into her shirtsleeve.

"Not right now," she whispered.

Tom pulled his arm back with a nervous chuckle. Seemingly, had had not even realized he was doing it, and he returned his attention to the stage.

Then it happened, very quickly. Her father's arm bumped the lectern, and a bit of him came off from the back of his hand, disintegrating into powder at his feet. Most of the audience hadn't noticed yet, but she could see the breaks in his skin, little fractures, like the dried-up pond behind their farmhouse in the summer. She felt Tom's arm twitch beside her. He opened his mouth. A word had caught in the back of his throat.

"No," she said, softly at first, then louder. "*No*."

Her father's entire stature crumbled, his jacket and trousers collapsing into a pile. Before she could stand, before she could even call to him, he had disappeared in a grayish cloud, leaving behind a mound of dust and crushed earth. The auditorium went silent, at first unsure what they had seen. Then, when she screamed, she let loose a crescendo of murmurs, sounds of shock, horror, and melancholy. Tom was standing next to her, reaching awkwardly for her shoulders, but when she looked him in the face, he seemed baffled.

A professor stood up from the third row, addressing her directly: "Did you know?"

"Did I *know*?" she said in anguish. "Know *what*?"

The professor gestured to the dust-pile on stage. "Did you know this was going to happen?"

"No!" she said, and broke into tears. "Are you saying—? But there was nothing I could do for him. I asked. There was nothing."

"No, no one's blaming you," Tom said gently.

"Yes, of course, girl, no one blames you," said the professor. "These men, they do this to themselves."

"No—" she said. "He didn't do this to himself either. That's not what happened." But already the faculty in the audience were conceding it, sharp, sad nods of assent breaking out in little tremors across the auditorium. Yes, he did it to himself, as men of the past often do. She tried again to protest, to defend her father, but she felt the force of this consensus hit her and carry her under like a wave. Students looked to their professors with anxiety, wanting desperately to leave but seeking direction as to how and whether they should. Somehow, she hated their squeamishness most of all. At least the disparaging professors, some of them coming to the ends of their careers, were willing to look at the dust-pile head-on. However, when the custodian came out with his broom—that was too much. With quiet groans, they looked away, and even she, his daughter, could not stand to watch the stage get swept.

There was only Tom now, her vibrant young athlete, her engineer, her chemist. She sat with him on the steps outside the auditorium, numb with grief, his damp handkerchief crumpled in her hand. There was still a great commotion around them, students and professors talking in quick voices about what had happened at the lecture. Tom's round face was still nonplussed. Several times, he seemed to attempt a profound statement, only to stop just short of saying it aloud. She could tell he wasn't used to being in a situation where no words seemed appropriate.

Eventually, he gave up on being profound and spoke timidly:

"I'm trying to remember what my father once told me, about the essential difference between women and men."

She looked up, observing his face through a fog of tears.

"He said—what was it he said?" Tom closed his eyes in concentration. "'Women are immortal through their children. Men are immortal through their legacy.' He said—that's why it's so important, what men make with their own hands here on earth."

She crumpled up the handkerchief, the pain of fresh tears knotting the back of her throat. "Do you think that's true?"

"I'm not sure," he said. "Maybe. I'm not sure." He saw her pained, wet eyes, staring him down. "My father said a lot in his day. It's probably nonsense."

But after this point, across many years, Tom's boundless energy would accelerate his career beyond measure. When she married him in his hometown of Dayton, Ohio, in the blistering heat of August, he would then be working for his father. Soon, he would switch over to General Motors, for whom he would invent a pivotal gasoline compound that would contribute to the rise of the auto industry and the deadly poisoning of many factory workers. He would contract polio in his fifties, become paralyzed, and accidentally strangle himself to death with the system of pulleys he devised to help get him out of bed in the morning. Carrying a tray of tea into his room, she would find him, their youngest away at Cornell, the eldest working for Lincoln Electric, the daughter married with a baby in Akron. Alone, she would find him.

Now, on the steps outside the auditorium, even in the wake of the tragedy he'd witnessed, she could feel his heart on fire, his yearning for the triumphs that would pave his way. As she sat in his light, she could feel her own dwindling. She could feel it stretching into a long day by the window, staring out.

Keepers

Now, here, you see, it takes all the running you can do,
to keep in the same place. If you want to get somewhere
else, you must run at least twice as fast as that!
—The Red Queen, *Through the Looking Glass*

When their father died, his house began to shift. To one sister it was growing larger, and to the other it was shrinking, and even though both of them could plainly tell this was happening, neither one said anything about it. Billie, the younger sister, thought she was imagining it, and so she wasn't immediately afraid. Margaret on the other hand, she was afraid from the start, but she wasn't about to tell anybody. She would take her fear and crunch it down and bury it, and that way nobody would ever experience the displeasure of seeing it.

There were other things to worry about anyway. As Margaret told Billie that morning on the drive over, the building inspector would be there at five and would surely condemn the place, maybe even write up some kind of citation, make them pay a fine. The house was in just that bad a state.

By all appearances, it was a handsome house, one of few remaining Victorian giants in a St. Louis suburb of postwar brick bungalows. But inside was a sickened labyrinth of narrow rooms and foul, dizzying smells. The foyer alone was nearly impassible, filled with waist-high stacks of magazines their father never read, meticulously organized bins of rusted hardware and engine parts, water-stained copies of the New Testament, the kind handed out by a plaintive door-to-door witness. The stairwell was piled with furniture, broken or half-made things he would've worked on a decade ago. It was obvious now that he hadn't been up to the second floor of the house in quite some time, having made his bed on a nest of macramé blankets in the sunroom.

Billie had thought Margaret was exaggerating when she said the house would be condemned, but now she stood in the doorway in shock.

"I didn't know it was this bad."

"How 'bout that," said Margaret.

"Where the hell do we even start?"

Billie turned to her sister, whose face had the look of a demure, gray-eyed falcon.

"We've got nine hours," Margaret said. "Obviously, we can only do so much, but if we at least get the garbage out from downstairs, that'll work in our favor."

Of course, Billie always knew their father hoarded, that it had gotten worse over the years. Last Thanksgiving, the whole Canby clan met up at the P.F. Chang's in Richmond Heights, and even their older brother Corwin had felt the need mention dad's "collections." It's really gotten to be a problem, he said. Someone should clear out all that *crap*.

Billie remembered that remark because it took all her strength to keep her eyes from rolling back in her head, because of course it didn't cross Corwin's mind that this task should fall to him, or that the disembodied *someone* he always spoke of was actually Margaret, a martyr of such practice you could practically see the arrows sticking out of her.

Now, a week after their father's funeral, Billie was grasping through a pile of mail by the door, trying to weed out the junk and the ad sheets from the payment notices and the parcels, things their father must've ordered online and had never opened. There was a mother-of-pearl end table buried under there somewhere, which had belonged to their mother.

"No!" Margaret snapped, snatching the papers from Billie's hands. "Absolutely not. You'll never get through like that. Never. Toss it all."

"But we don't know what all is in here yet," Billie said.

"Right, see there," said her sister, "you're getting distracted already. I told you you'd get distracted. If you really want to be useful, go get the trash bags from the truck."

Billie dropped her arms to her side.

"Mags. We talked about this. I am here to help. Here I am."

Margaret's watery falcon eyes cut through her. She took off her glasses and let them dangle on the beaded chain around her neck, as if Billie had been the one to leave the house in such a humiliating state, as if Billie had done it all on purpose.

"You want me to be nice?"

"Nice would be a good start," said Billie.

"Okay. If you really want to be useful, stop looking through every little piece of mail and *please* go get the trash bags from the truck."

Yes. This was how it was going to be. Margaret: stalking away down the narrow path their father had carved in the refuse. Billie: retreating out into the front yard with her hands pressed to her temples. Corwin wasn't there. He and his wife and kids were four hours away at their cabin in the Ozarks. They had removed themselves from under the weight of their father's death, and they had told Margaret to do the same. Leave the house until after, Corwin said. It's too soon.

But of course it hadn't happened like that. Billie was stuck here, helping, fantasizing about what she'd do if her sister went off like she had at their father's eightieth birthday party, how she could just take the truck and leave (it was her truck, after all; Margaret drove so seldom now she had let her license expire). Fourteen hours on the road and she'd be back in Wilmington with Mayfair, her six-toed lover—she could make it in a day if she didn't sleep—and *that* would surely fit everyone's assumptions about the youngest

child, the fitful adopted one, the Chinese lesbian. The one
who'd moved so many places, been so many different people,
that now—boyish, wintery-haired, forty-five—the memories
of the seventeen years she'd occupied this awful house
seemed to belong to someone else.

It was warm outside, a late spring heat, the
neighborhood humming with a wakeful greenness. Billie
took her time grabbing up the stuff from the back of the
truck. Then, when she headed back inside, she noticed there
was something odd about the doorway.

With a box of garbage bags in one hand, rubber gloves
in the other, she held out her arms to either side and rested
her knuckles on the jamb. It was wider, wasn't it? Maybe
she could say it was wider than she remembered from her
childhood. Maybe she could assume that the door had
been replaced since she'd left home. But no. She had the
unshakable feeling that the door was wider than it had
been just seconds ago, when she came out to get bags from
the truck.

Funny, she thought. The mind is funny.

Margaret leaned into the foyer, a tower of *Guidepost*
magazines in her arms. She saw Billie standing there.

"What are you doing?"

"Just helping you, Mags," said Billie.

Margaret did not blink. She seldom did.

"Come on. I've got a pile started."

Margaret's tactic was to keep moving, back and forth to
the trash-pile altar she was building in the living room.
She tried to disregard the image of her sister standing in
the doorway, arms out as if measuring the distance. Could
she see it too? Margaret had seen it as soon as they pulled
up in the driveway. She'd cleaned off her glasses with her
shirtsleeve to make sure it wasn't a trick of the light, but
upon walking through the front door, of course, yes. The
last time she'd been here, it had taken thirteen paces to
get from the foyer to the living room. Now it took only
twelve.

The inspector would be appalled: How did you let the place get this way? How could you let a man live in a shrinking house?

She trusted that getting the junk out would fix this problem. Trash first. All the old dailies and journals, some damp and soiled to the point of pulp. Rotting food in the refrigerator, mouse-eaten crackers in the pantry, birdseed sprouting in plastic containers, a sticky fruit bowl overtaken by ants. Pitiful and revolting, an enemy scourge. Margaret was not thinking about what they would do with things they might want to keep. (Would she want to keep anything at all?) She didn't let herself think that far ahead. Trash on pile. That's what we're doing right now.

As she worked, she fought the idea that their father was somehow still in the house with them, refused to entertain that pagan nonsense, ghosts and spirits and whatnot. The man was dead. He had entered the Lord's Kingdom.

Even so, she couldn't help but feel that when they ventured into the sunroom, they would find he'd taken up his usual spot on the nest of blankets, sorting different sized washers into containers while the old box television blared a shrill program about whalers in the North Pacific. Such was how she'd found him a couple weeks ago, when she and Corwin—they both lived in Warrenton, an hour away—came in for a visit. Odd how you could live so near a person and rarely see them, rarely want to see them. She'd brought a box of cheese crackers and Hostess cakes. Plus fruit. He didn't eat enough fruit. And the whole ride over in Corwin's Subaru, she jiggled the box on her knees.

"You know we're enabling him," Corwin said. "We come and go, and we don't say anything about the state of the house. He says he buys forty useless spark plugs from Mr. Richter's garage at two cents a pop, and we say wow, Dad, what a deal."

"It's not our place to tell him how to keep his home," said Margaret. She could already feel a prickling rash breaking out on her neck. "But if you want to be the one to tell him to clean up, go ahead."

Corwin said nothing. In the silence, Margaret took a
Hostess cake from the box, unwrapped it, and stuffed it
in her mouth.

"Sometimes tough love is the best love," said her
brother.

Margaret agreed. But when it came to their father, their
love was anxious and quiet and placating. Each time, as if
by enchantment, she would pass through the door of the
house, and her soul would close up like a telescope,
transforming her into the brittle creature she'd been as a
girl, and Corwin would become a song-and-dance man,
eager for a light-hearted chats about college ball. Even as
middle-aged adults, they could not stand up to their father,
seated on his blankets in a tartan robe, an aged giant
organizing his domain. He regarded them with such
distrust, the way he inspected each of Margaret's treats,
as if to check for tampering.

"I wish you'd quit trying to feed me this," he told her,
setting the fruit aside. "It just brings the ants in."

Margaret clenched the cake wrapper in her pocket with
sticky fingers. Corwin didn't see, but when they left, she
threw it into one of the junk piles in the living room.

She was walking to work at the library when she learned
about the stroke. One of her father's neighbors called, said
she'd gone over to the house to help get rid of a wasp nest.
He hadn't recognized her. His left arm hung dead at his
side. Four days followed of sterile, hospital smells, grim
correspondence, grim prayers, physicians and nurses doing
their jobs with virtuous efficiency, Billie riding up in her
truck wearing stained sneakers and a backpack like an
adolescent vagrant, Corwin returning out of breath from
a conference in Minneapolis, as if he'd jogged the whole
way. Then, on day five, their father was dead, and Margaret
was left with a strange memory of walking down the green-
tiled hallway, hospice room to nurse's station, her loafers
hovering an inch above the ground.

Now, tearing through their father's things, she was
angry that she had allowed all this cancerous clutter to

grow, angry that she hadn't stood before him and said enough is enough. I'm tearing down your fortress. I'm unburdening your heart. . .

Where was Billie? Her sister had filled up three trash bags, hurled them out into the yard and disappeared. And the inspector was coming. What a mess, Ms. Canby. He'd see it all.

Margaret squeezed past walls of old books and VHS tapes. She ducked her head when she entered the kitchen (she'd always been a tall woman but had never needed to do that), and there was Billie in the sunroom, sitting cross-legged on the floor, surrounded by boxes of garbage. It was one of those times when she looked to Margaret like a fifteen-year-old boy.

"It's all pretty organized, considering," said Billie. "This one's just old keys. That's a box of dog toys. Did he get a dog?"

"No," said Margaret. "He didn't like animals."

"What was he going to do with all this?"

"He had plans to sell it."

Billie had also found a shoebox filled with necklaces. In fact, she was now wearing a hemp cowry-shell choker.

"Mayfair will enjoy this." She beamed. "Circa 1999! Can't be mine, but I had one like it, exchanged it for a special brownie at a neighborhood yard sale and I think I got the better end of the deal. Oh—hello, what's this now?" Within the knot of chains and rhinestones, Billie extracted a string of blue beads marked with Asian characters.

"You think he could've picked this up for our mother in China?" she asked.

"It's probably from the flea market," said Margaret.

Billie lifted the beads toward Margaret, offering them to her.

"I don't want them," she said. "I never wear flashy jewelry."

"You'd rather just throw them out?"

Margaret's low voice settled in the air like smoke, measured and hazardous: "Billie, this was *not* what we were doing. You've gotten distracted."

Billie gazed up at her towering sister, looking ever more hawkish in the sunroom's tarnished yellow light. Of course, it was all shit. Tons of shit, selected, handled, sorted, stashed and kept, all with a level of loving attention Billie had never known their father to express otherwise.

"What do you really want to do, Billie?" Margaret asked her. "Do you want to sit here and go through necklaces, or do you want to help me?"

Billie wanted to do the former, but she could see the hardened gray stone in Margaret's eyes, which, ever since they were children, had always been the first sign of trouble.

She knew what it was like to watch her sister unravel.

Was his birthday party really the last time she saw him? That was over a year ago at Corwin's house in Warrenton, though it was Margaret who'd put herself in charge. Billie assumed it would be awkward; since neither sister had a husband or children, all their older relatives could do was remark on the obvious, how the Canby daughters were all grown up, how they used to see them in church as little girls, quiet Margaret May and feisty Wilhelmina Louise. Maybe they would bring up the time their father removed them from Sunday service and spanked them in the narthex. Maybe they would ask about Billie's travels abroad. Some of them, eager to exhibit their tolerance and progressivism, might mention Liz, Billie's longtime partner. How was she? How was all that going? And Billie would say that things were fine rather than the truth, which was that she and Liz had broken up three years ago.

But Margaret didn't leave much time for Billie to socialize, having assigned her with a series of party tasks. Disinfect the lawn furniture. Refill the coffee dispenser. Load pictures onto this electronic photo frame. Go out on the deck and light those Chinese lanterns.

"Why do you want *me* to light the Chinese lanterns?" Billie scoffed, feigning indignation. "You think that'll make them more authentic?"

And their father and Corwin and Corwin's preteen daughter all laughed, but Margaret only hardened and looked ready to thrust her hand onto the grill in anguish.

It was true that Billie stuck with Corwin that day. She found comfort there, hiding out in the basement to watch a ball game. Then the thunderstorm came. Hailstones shredded the Chinese lanterns. Guests grabbed up their gifts and dishware and pressed their damp bodies into the house. When Billie came back upstairs for a beer, it was as if she'd stumbled into a Red Cross tent in the heart of a national disaster. Someone was shouting—"Did *nobody* think to grab the brats, for God's sake?"—and Margaret, for one reason or another, began to cry. That was when Billie overheard their father saying to a fellow church deacon: "I don't get it. I told her I didn't want it, this whole thing, but she went and did it anyway." He caught Billie's eye and spoke to her. "Do *you* get it?"

Billie was surprised that he'd asked her for her opinion. Had he ever done that? It was easy to believe that he simply didn't like her, that he'd always favored his biological children, that since their mother died, Billie was just a missionary project gone wrong. But here he wanted her opinion, and she gave him the one she thought he'd prefer.

"No. I don't get it."

"Maggie should've gotten married," her father went on. "She's got too much energy, spends it on nonsense like this."

Later, when they were sitting on the guest bedroom floor together, her sister's face swollen and sleepy, Billie pried her:

"Why *did* you go to all the effort? I mean, if he said he didn't want it. . ."

"But he did want it," Margaret said. Her voice sounded as though it had been filed down, like the metal dust was still in there. "Or—maybe I just imagined he did. I really don't know. God bless me if I could explain it to you, this need—like if I could just crack him open—"

Margaret laughed.

"That sounds awful. So violent."

In the weeks to follow, Billie wondered if Margaret had planned the damn party because she knew it would fail, that something about all that prickly family wreckage kept her nourished, kept her moving. Their father had built a whole house on wreckage. Billie could see that now.

After finding the string of beads in the sunroom, she kept them in her pocket as a talisman to protect her against the rest of the house. Margaret was right that they were probably from a flea market, but Billie liked to imagine her adoptive parents street shopping in Beijing among the heathens. Now, whenever she moved from one room to another, distances widened. The ceilings stretched high overhead. They resembled the vaulted cathedrals she'd toured in France and Italy, when she told Liz those places made her feel like Jonah trapped in the belly of the whale, and Liz had interpreted that as a metaphor for their relationship. As the sun moved into the afternoon, blades of light broke through the dusty windows and sliced into the landscape of their father's things. Her footsteps echoed.

Margaret was still a flurry of activity. They hadn't even paused to eat anything.

At one point, Billie gripped her sleeve.

"There's no way we'll get all this done by five today, Mags."

"Not with *your* work ethic," said Margaret.

"We have to start in on the stairwell, get it cleared out. The inspector's gonna need to get up to the second floor."

"No, we had a plan. First floor trash, then the stairs."

"We may not have *time.*"

She let word ring in the air—*time, time.* Five o'clock, the inspector had said on the phone, bright and chipper. Margaret scowled. She looked toward the ceiling, toward the stairs, where a line of black ants was snaking its way up the banister.

She never said Billie was right, but then, she never did. They just set to work, moving the obstruction, piece by piece, from the stairs to the front porch, the tangled rungs and slats of unfinished furniture, cans of sanding solution and varnish, heavy plastic tarps, yellowed and strangely wet. By now, Billie was beginning to hurt, a familiar pain that started in her lower back and fanned out over her shoulders.

With sweaty fingers, she scrambled for a solid grip on the back of a half-upholstered armchair, which their father had left on the landing. The fabric smelled rotten-sweet, like spoiled fruit.

"Haul up your end," said Margaret. Billie could see her biceps. Had she always been so strong?

"It's slipping. You've got longer arms than me."

"Come on, Billie, dear. Didn't you take boxing lessons? Haul it up now or it'll drop down the stairs."

She took a breath and mustered her strength. How irritating that this had been her idea.

"We need to turn it," said Margaret. "That foot's sticking out, it'll hit the wall and get stuck."

"It won't get stuck. There's plenty of room."

"I tell you, it's going to hit the wall, Bill."

"And so what if it does? So what?" She shifted the armchair's weight onto her shoulders, which sparked with sudden pain.

"Billie, don't you have eyes? Turn the chair so it doesn't hit the wall."

"Mags, it's miles away, it's fine, stop shouting."

The bannister shuddered. Somewhere in the house, a jar fell off a shelf and broke. Billie opened her flinching eyes and saw that foot of the armchair had punctured the drywall. Margaret made a small scream, as if she'd been stabbed.

"Pull back, pull back," Billie cried, and they heaved the chair up a step, wrenching it free in a cloud of gray dust. From inside the tear-shaped hole, a nest of ants spilled like smoke, the tiny creatures tumbling over one another's bodies, white larvae in their jaws. By the time the sisters brought their load to the foot of the stairs, the ants were on them, crawling down their bare arms and into their shoes. They could feel them biting.

"Fucking Christ!" said Billie.

There in the foyer, she shook them off, kicking away her sandals so she could pinch them out from between her toes.

But Margaret couldn't shake them off. She didn't have room. Everywhere she turned, she hit a wall. There was no choice but to push past Billie and burst out through the front door, to jump and thrash in the front yard. Neighbors rode by and saw her, a middle-aged woman, lost in the throes of what looked like a religious fit.

No, Margaret never married. There was always too much to do, and she just never got around to it. It was the same with leaving town, her father's town, every sight and street thick with childhood dreaming, and her house, the one she'd saved for, alone, with no one else, just six miles away from where her father lived. Where would she go if she left? You didn't become a better person by running.

Not to say she wasn't jealous of Corwin and his family, or Billie, taking off the way she did. Fresh out of high school, and there she went, stealing six hundred dollars out of their father's lockbox (she did pay it back eventually). Even if Margaret approved, she could never have done something so bold. She'd have gotten caught, and she would've repented.

Then time passed, and the postcards started coming in—Atlanta, Philadelphia, Manhattan—then, over the years, more extravagant places—Montreal, Dublin, Florence, Paris, remote cities like Reykjavik, which she'd never even heard of before. Sometimes, Billie sent pictures of the people she traveled with, a crew of white twenty-somethings with dirty hair and shining faces. In her thirties, this group whittled down to a single mannish, wiry woman. Margaret was no fool; she knew what this meant. She was four years older and could see her sister clearly, and you could even say she'd known since she they were children and thought it ungodly, though someone who lived that far away wasn't asking for approval.

Billie ended up making her home base in Eastern North

Carolina, where she got her associate's in sociology and started work for a non-profit, some environmental whatnot. Margaret called her about once a month.

"Do you think you'll go to China?" she asked once.

"Can't go anywhere right now," said Billie. "Liz and me are cleaned out."

"But do you think you'll go eventually?"

Margaret had a strange, fearful thought that Billie would travel there, find her birth parents and never be heard from again.

"Hasn't really interested me," said Billie. "Maybe one day."

Now, at their father's house, Margaret sat on the porch steps, scratching at the swollen bites on her ankles. Billie got some bottled water and a container of painkillers from her truck.

"For the bites?" asked Margaret.

"No," said Billie. "My back and shoulders."

"You're sore already?"

"Osteoarthritis. In my forties, I know, whoopee, and all this white in my hair, more every year. Blame genetics, I guess."

She sat next to Margaret.

"I could use a beer. Or three."

Margaret was quiet, playing with her beaded eyeglass chain.

"Bill," she said, "I don't think I want to go up there yet. I'll just keep on with the first floor, and come join you in an hour or so."

"Okay," said Billie. "We can do that."

They stared at the lawn, which was filled with trash bags. Neither of them was thinking of anything important; Billie was realizing how much she missed those huge elm trees that used to guard this street, and Margaret was remembering the games she'd played with Billie, how fast and clever her little sister was, how well she could hide, even as a toddler. It was she who'd found the loose panel behind Margaret's closet, an unreachable hiding space. Kept it secret for the longest time.

Margaret broke the silence.

"Was this place really so bad?" she asked. "So bad that you had to run away? Did you hate Dad so much that you had to break his heart like that?"

Billie turned to her sister, heart sinking. She wondered maybe if she just ignored the question, Margaret would move on, but she didn't.

"Well—all right. If you don't want to answer me, that's fine. In the end, we only answer to one, and He loves us no matter what. And Dad loved you, even though your choices broke his heart."

Billie wasn't surprised, but it still hurt. It always hurt when Margaret took a swipe out of nowhere, as senseless as an impulse to spit.

"No," said Billie. "No, Mags, I won't get into this. Dad wasn't kind to me, to any of us, but me in particular, and it's weird that you keep wanting to rewrite history. But I won't get into it."

Margaret looked at her with wet eyes. "He did his best."

"I won't get into it," Billie said again. "No."

"You never want to have an honest conversation with me."

She laughed bitterly. "An *honest conversation*. Are you serious?"

"Leave me alone then. If you don't want to talk, leave me alone."

Billie pressed her face into her hands. She was still so quick to anger, so sensitive. Mayfair knew that. Mayfair had told her to stay in North Carolina, but she hadn't listened.

The stairs gave Billie some trouble. Each step was so wide and high she found herself using her hands to pull herself along. She and her sister had gotten everything cleared from the stairwell except a bundle of soiled rugs and a pile of coat racks, which blocked the way like ramparts. One by one, she hauled them up and let them tumble to the landing.

In the upstairs hallway, she began to see things she remembered: vast walls lined with cupboards and curio cabinets, each shelf packed with porcelain breakables—sheep and shepherds, Jesus with the little children, women of the French court, feminine and sacred. These had belonged to their mother, a compulsive collector in her own right. The bittersweet smell of rot hung in the air, and though Billie had brought along a trash bag, she kept her arms at her side and touched nothing. The sight of the place hushed and awed her, and above it all she could still feel the ugly ache Margaret had left behind. She didn't want to be anywhere near her sister.

Liz had asked about family. So had Mayfair. She'd told them both stories about a tyrant king who preferred his natural-born children, about his adopted stable-hand, the one who was never quite modest enough, or studious enough, or grateful enough, and who fucked other girls at church camp. Mayfair was ten years Billie's junior and had been raised by bona-fide Village artists; that a parent could so reject their child was a tragedy as foreign to her as honor killings. Sometimes, Billie found herself drinking the girl's happiness, as she had on their recent trip down to the tide pools at Fort Fisher, how her bare, freakish feet gripped the rocks, polydactyl, like Hemingway's cats, how she shined with light when she touched the anemones and watched them recoil into their stony hideaways. Billie and this golden lover were cleaning the sand off their feet when they got the call from Margaret about their father.

"You really have to go back to Missouri?" Mayfair asked.

"Margaret says he's dying."

"I'll go with you."

"That's sweet to offer, doll, but I know it'll be best for everyone if I go by myself."

Mayfair's glow dimmed. When she wasn't glowing, she was like a child, petulant and careless. "I just hate it," she said. "I hate that you keep subjecting yourself to your sister."

Billie continued on to her old bedroom, which was crammed with hope chests and wicker furniture, heaped toward a ceiling so high they seemed to dissolve into shadow. A big stack of LPs blocked the closet, which was partly open, overflowing with an intestinal heap of shirts and scarves. And while all her old toys were still here, a coat of dust had increased their size, giving them their own sinister life. What did she think she would find here? An answer? A childhood song? *Oh Maggie I couldn't have tried anymore. . .*

Margaret's room was next door, but Billie got distracted. There was a turn at the end of the hallway. She didn't remember it being there. An addition? For how long now? Who lived in these rooms? The way her footsteps echoed off the walls, she could imagine that she was the first to ever enter this part of the house.

Her mind kept coming back here. Her heart kept returning to Margaret.

Meanwhile, in the downstairs foyer, Margaret was staring up the dark tunnel on the stairwell. A weaker woman would feel sorry, but she did not feel sorry. She refused to give Billie praise for the most basic act of decency. Help your sister. Stay.

"Billie," Margaret called.

No answer.

"Billie, don't play games."

In the resounding silence, Margaret hunched her shoulders and began making her way up the stairs. She barely fit, and she was furious to find the landing choked with rubbish. The arm of a broken coat rack snagged her eyeglass chain and snapped it off her neck. The beads flew away, vanished forever.

"Damn it." It was the first time she'd cursed aloud in years.

In the upstairs hall, she squeezed sideways past their mother's old cabinets. Their father's door was behind her, but she didn't turn around, kept moving forward. Billie's room then hers, it went like that. Corwin got the big room on the third floor because he was the boy.

"Billie?"

Her bedroom door was open, but there was no way anyone could fit in there. Margaret kept on, her chin tucked to her chest.

How long since she'd been up here? She wasn't one to wax sentimental about the past so it must've been years, not that she harbored regrets either. She didn't begrudge their father his collecting, or his strict hand, a rough, warm hand from a farming family, God's people, that was just their way. And wasn't he a good man, after all? A good man who'd done his best in the absence of a mother Margaret lost when she was six?

She had wanted to be a good daughter, good Christian, but too slow and helpless to be anything else. As a child lying in bed at night, afraid of shadows, it was always Bible verses, whispered aloud, that gave her comfort: *For if ye forgive men their trespasses, your heavenly Father will also forgive you.* She could remember the crack in her ceiling, which had been a point of fixation, how she had watched that crack snake its way from one side of the room to the other.

Her neck burned. She was breaking out in one of her rashes. All around, the walls wedged her into the hallway between Billie's room and hers, and she could no longer move forward. Realizing this, she twisted around to turn back, tried to reposition her arms but found them pinned to her side, and the walls in the opposite direction presenting her with the same problem. The building inspector was on his way. He would find her, humiliated, crushed by her own father's house. He would condemn their house. He would condemn her.

She blinked tearfully in the dim light, then took in a dusty breath and screamed.

Elsewhere, Billie heard her. She was moving through a wide passageway she didn't recognize, listening for footsteps. For a while, she convinced herself they were hers, just an echo, but now she recalled the heavy night-stride of their father, the weight of his voice, the strength of his grip, and marks, imprints the color of plums. Margaret. The building inspector was coming, but Billie was starting to think he'd already been there, a stout man in a tie, with an official pen from an agency, asking her if she enjoyed where she was living, asking her if she had seen anything in the house, heard anything, and she had said she was very happy, and they were all very happy.

"Billie! Billie!"

She heard Margaret's voice, breaking with panic. Where was she?

"Bill, help me, I've gotten myself stuck."

She listened. Where was the voice was coming from? Up ahead? At the end the passage she found a doorway, what turned out be the false panel in the back of Margaret's closet, her old hiding space. Margaret's room, Margaret's things, all of it lying quiet with dust.

"Billie, where are you?"

"Here," she cried. And she was, and her sister was just on the other side of the wall.

One for Sorrow, Two for Joy

Vic, I send out so many thoughts toward you that you may never hear. But ever since we had that argument about your mother, and the Bi-Lo checkout girl saw you wandering out past the train tracks on the other side of the Business Loop, and the police dredged your backpack out of the rock quarry, our world has gone all still and fuzzy like those paintings you loved so much. Remember? The ones of lonely people sitting in hotel rooms and restaurants? Who was that painter, Vic? Hodgson? Hooper? Anyway, thing is, your sister is collecting again. It's becoming a problem.

Do you know what my life is like now, Vic? I drive home from Middlebury—yes, I'm still the secretary at your old elementary school, stuffy Aunt Alice, ordinary as a pigeon. I drive home to the apartment you hated, and that Marcie hates still, an apartment in a treeless complex surrounded on all sides by power lines and traffic and auto sale lots. I know it's ugly as homemade soap. I've always known that, don't you kids fool yourselves into thinking it's dull people that make dull places and not the other way around.

But where is Marcie finding this stuff, really? The antlers I can understand—there's dead deer by the side of the road all over town. But the quartz crystals? The rat skulls? The lotus pods? It's positively *pagan*. Yesterday, Mrs. Schuman, the landlady, came over and saw one of Marcie's arrangements all laid out on the coffee table—particular-like, you know the way she does it, like she's trying to summon Beelzebub to our living room. Then Mrs. Schuman put on this mask of feigned concern, all, She's sixteen now, isn't she? This is something a younger child would do, one who still plays make-believe.

I had to pretend like it didn't bother me.

Now, it's been over a year since you disappeared. Of course Marcie suffers in your absence, and I'd never say she can't hope or grieve or scream. I've told her she can scream at me, but she won't. I've told her she can curse the Lord God, but she won't. She just collects. She amasses. She won't talk to anyone. Won't make friends. Doesn't reach out to her teachers. She's failing school because she skips to go off on these searches, and she brings her stuff back here, and she sets it up in little patterns, little arrangements, little messes, so that if I want to use the coffee table, I have to tell her to move it. I have to say, Marcie, you know we're sharing this apartment together.

You used to tell me not to hold her weirdness against her. God knows the two of you were always weird children and that's just how you are. But Vic, we're sharing this apartment, this world, we are sharing it *together*, and I feel like Marcie doesn't even think of me. I can stand in front of her and it's like I'm not even there.

Say, do you remember that little red book you gave Marcie, the one you found at the secondhand shop by the Soap'n'Suds? It was someone Feinlein—*The Numinous Mass of Objects*, that was it. It's nothing occult is it, Vic? She always has it with her and she must've read it a hundred times now—it was tattered before, and now the spine is holding on by threads. I asked once if I could see it, but she just gave this tight little shrug, said it was for *science*. She's never had an interest in science before, maybe that's a good thing.

Vic, I wish you could tell me if I'm overreacting about this collection. It's mostly just that it's an eyesore I have to stare at in my own home, but if I'm honest, it's not hurting me any. Maybe Marcie should just *have* the coffee table, for pity's sake, and the china cabinet in the dining room and the steamer trunk in the hall, and the kitchen counter. Not like I need the counter space anyway. I never cook anymore; we're always ordering Chinese nowadays and I don't even care for Chinese.

I *will* need to say something about the cattails (where did she get cattails?). She wove them like a garland around the porch railing, and when the sun hits them in the afternoon, they smell eggy and rotten.

I've been thinking a lot lately about how I never understood you kids, you and Marcie, how close you were. I was outside looking in the whole time. Did you know the school counselor once came to me all concerned? Yes, Vic. It was some years ago. Marcie was in second grade and you were in fifth, and the school counselor caught me as I was leaving the office, wanted to tell me she was worried the two of you weren't making friends with kids your age, that you were too attached to each other—that you were too close. You can imagine what I said. Piss off, Paula, they just lost their mother. Of course, I said it with the tact of a lady, but you get the idea.

Now I can't help but see that your absence has left Marcie at a disadvantage. As I said, she never has friends over, hardly says a word to anyone at school, no interest in movies or music or boys. I would say she talks to me, but even that feels strained, like we just barely speak each other's languages. She's so lonely, Vic. She's wrapped herself up in her loneliness, you can feel it, and now it's like that's all she knows.

Anyway. I'm all vexed lately. It's something she said about you. You and the collection.

◆ ◆ ◆

Christ in heaven, the collection.

You know it's beginning to really stink? Not surprising. Been a month since all this started and some of the stuff is rotting—crab shells, seaweed, skate egg cases. She found maybe a hundred Japanese beetles, iridescent green, the kind that'll decimate your roses, and now she's pinned them up on the wall in her room like constellations. They're rotting too. And on my way to the toilet last night, my poor bare feet got all torn up on some tiny shells she'd arranged in spirals on the carpet in the hall. They were— what'dya call it—periwinkles. With little sea creatures molding away inside, stinking to high heaven.

So the next morning I interrupted Marcie's 101st read of *The Numinous Mass of Objects*. I looked her straight in the eye. You need to start keeping all this stuff confined to your room, I said. You can have it, it can be your little thing, but only in *your* space. Not in *other people's* spaces. There are two people living in this apartment.

She just stared at me, not angry, not upset, like she expected as much. But at least she was listening. At least I had her eyes a minute. So I asked her then. We are miles from any marshland. We are miles from any ocean. We live in a concrete box in a scourge of urban sprawl. Marcie, I said, where are you *getting* this stuff?

And she said she got it from you.

From Vic, I said. You got it from Vic.

And something stirred in me then, something like hope, like an old belief in magic. They never found you, after all. They fished your backpack from the water at the bottom of the quarry, but they could never say for sure that you'd drowned. I took Marcie by the shoulders and shook her, and her face flinched, as if I'd just spat in it, but I was trying—really—I was just trying to reach in, pull her out.

Marcie, I said, do you know where Vic is?

Her face crumpled. She started crying. I was glad to see her cry—no, that sounds wrong. I was glad that she could cry in front of me, that she could share some emotion, whatever was going on with this searching and hoarding and arranging, that she could share something with *me*.

She said, Vic's gone. She said, Vic's not coming back.

And since then. . .

Since then, she's done as I asked. She gathered all her stuff and hid it away inside her bedroom, cleared it off the coffee table, cleared it off the china cabinet and the steamer trunk and the kitchen counter. Now she won't say anything else about it, and she stays all closed up in her room, and it's almost like I've got the apartment all to myself.

Your mother was an actress. I say that, even though she never made it as a professional actress, she still was an actress in spirit. I remember seeing her in a school play when she was Marcie's age. *Inherit the Wind*, the one about the monkey trials. There were not enough boys taking drama, so she played the Mencken character, the smooth-talking journalist. She ambled across the stage in a straw hat and suspenders, sucking the juices from a bright red apple. Not a subtle portrayal. Nor a very convincing one. But I can remember watching her, and I felt this flame of jealousy, seeing her up there, carrying around a glow she'd had since she was a little kid, what obvious pleasure she took in performing. I was jealous, and then I felt stupid for being jealous, because I was six years older than your mother. I had a job. I had a fiancé. Granted, he was a man without much ambition who sold heaters, not a bad man, but a humorless man who preferred the house to be dead silent, and who never failed to find something to complain about when he ordered food at restaurants. Granted, I ended up telling myself I could do better.

Sometimes, you can't do better.

I guess what I've been trying to grapple with, Vic, is that when we had our fight that last day you were home, and I said I was the best mother you had, it was not to say that you were better off living with your fat pigeon spinster aunt. It wasn't to say that your mother had abandoned you, or that it was her fault for disappearing, as you have now disappeared. It was to say that sometimes you have to work with what you're dealt, and sometimes that isn't much. When it all comes down to it, you have to accept that things are not as happy or exciting as you might like. That things are just okay. And well, I know you'd hate to hear me say this, Vic, but sometimes okay is better than nothing.

Somewhere is better than Nowhere.

What is wrong with your sister? The other day, she dragged in this whole mess of briars and branches into her bedroom, scratched the walls all to hell. At least now I think I've found out what she's building—some kind of shell, or a nest maybe. It looks like she's crawling in there to sleep at night.

The neighbors are what made me intervene. See, I guess I didn't realize how bad the smell had gotten, because I was startled and embarrassed to see Mrs. Schuman show up with a little crew—Mr. Patchett and his wife, and the bank teller who lives in the apartment to our left, I forget her name now, and Mr. Carstairs, the mush-mouthed fellow who lives below us. This crew appeared at the door, their eyes shifting with embarrassment as though they would rather be anywhere else. They let Mrs. Schuman do all the talking.

We're just mildly concerned, Alice, she said. Marcie is a special girl. And Vic—we know what happened with Vic must have been hard on her. On both of you. But. . .

The smell can hardly be *that* bad, I said.

It's pretty bad, they said.

Then we went down the hall to Marcie's room, and I opened the door, and the stink was so intense, so physical, that it knocked us back against the opposite wall. We all caught a glimpse of the nest, woven like a great, thorny cave around the spot where her bed used to be. It took up half the room. I shouted Marcie's name and told her to come out, and she, from inside the nest, shouted back that she was busy. Can you picture it? Our neighbors were just standing there, Vic. They were standing right there next to me with their hands and shirt collars over the noses, staring about the room. They must have been marveling at how badly I've failed this girl.

I'm not proud of what I did next. In my defense, I truly was mortified, angrier than I'd been in a long time. I tore my way into the room, crunching shells and twigs and things underfoot. Marcie heard that and caught on fast about what I was doing. She cried out—Stop! You'll wreck it!—but I was already reaching my arm into the mouth of the nest. There she was, all wide-eyed, tucked away in the belly of this hideous thing she'd built. She had a flashlight in one hand and *The Numinous Mass of Objects* in the other. When I grabbed the book, I wasn't gentle. Maybe I was even hoping it would tear apart, and that its destruction would bring her back to this world, or at least to a place we could live in together. Because it did tear apart, right there, right along the spine. Pages scattered. Marcie let out a shriek and threw herself at me. She was always a quiet child, and suddenly she was more animal than human. Suddenly she was a monster who sleeps in a nest, screaming—Never! You'll never! You'll never!

Never what, Vic?

Sometimes, I admit, it has crossed my mind that the two of you are changelings.

You liked folktales, fairy tales and all that. You probably knew about changelings. The fairies would come in the night and steal a child, and they'd leave one of their own in its place. Sort of like how the cuckoo tricks other birds into raising its young.

Was that you? Were you a cuckoo?

Of course, I say *were* now as if I'm sure you'll never come back. If you do come back, save your sister. She's bound to get crushed under the weight of this place.

I can't make much sense of Reiner Feinlein. But then, he wrote this book in 1968 and they were all on drugs then. He really likes black holes. He goes on and on about them. They crush light. I'm sure you already knew that. They're so powerful, they crush light.

I thought Marcie would've written more notes or highlighted or some such, but she's left the book mostly untouched. There's only one passage underlined, and I can't even tell if it was Marcie. Maybe it was the previous owner. *An object's Real Mass (RM) is determined by both physical presence (density) and emotional meaning (numinosity). No object in the universe exists without meaning. As the dying star pierces spacetime with its density, so too can a highly numinous arrangement break through the structured confines of physical existence.*

Nineteen sixty-eight. Did you know, Vic? That was the same year I was born.

The police told me Marcie ran away. They're looking for her on the edge of town. They're checking the bus stations, the railroad tracks, the quarry where they found your backpack. But I know. At least—I know more than they do.

I haven't been able to tell anyone what happened. For a while, I'd even convinced myself I witnessed nothing. See, after Marcie and I fought and the neighbors left, I stayed up until four a.m. hot gluing that damned book back together again. I wanted to give it to Marcie the next morning, to apologize. I drifted off in the easy chair in the living room, imagining this moment. In my dreams it went beautifully. We were both calm. We both understood each other perfectly.

So you were asleep, the police said. So she could've snuck out.

I said I probably would've heard her and woken up.

Maybe she climbed out the window, down the drainpipe?

Maybe. Sure. Yes, that's what must've happened.

But my mind keeps going back to that morning, again and again. The glare from the sun woke me up around eight. The hot glue gun was still plugged in, dripping from its nozzle. *The Numinous Mass of Objects* was gone.

Down the hall, her bedroom door was open, exposing her collection to the world. It really is a marvel, more so than I'd thought. She'd woven animal bones into reeds and vines, had built a wall out of bounded-up bundles of lichen and mistletoe and seaweed. There were stones and seashells all over the floor, arranged like—what do you call them?—fractals. Like fractals. Spinning and swirling. They made me dizzy.

Vic, I was afraid to go in, afraid of what I'd see. I heard a sound coming from inside the nest, a sort of humming or buzzing, like old TVs used to do when you turned them off. I called Marcie's name. Did I really think she'd answer?

There was a hole inside the nest.

Not in the *nest*, rather. In the air. There was a hole in the air. Three feet wide. Three feet tall. It opened into a black, chilly space and was surrounded by a grainy film, something like static, which made it seem only half there. I could smell the ocean drifting out of it. I could smell a marsh.

I waited a long time.

Then, when I finally reached my arm through the mouth of the nest, the hole came alive. It shuddered and spun. I drew back, afraid.

Was that it, Vic? Was that my chance? It's not something I could tell anyone about if it was. It's not like I could direct them through to follow you. If that was my opening—and really, am I fooling myself to think it was meant for me at all?—I never would've taken it. There's no way. Not even in my dreams. All I could do was crouch there, stock-still, as that hole flickered and spun. It spun so fast that it shrank down to nothing, and then it winked away.

Stereograms

Gail's husband, Nick, used to teach photography at a community college. Every fall, he and Gail and a makeshift crew of college friends would go out to the woods around Raleigh and shoot a horror movie to submit to the amateur film festival in October. They would come home again with their clothes ruined, covered in all that fake blood, white face putty and oil drippage from the chainsaws without chains. In the five years they were married, Nick made an unwilling actress of Gail. He beheaded her, gouged her, strangled her. He laid her down in an icy pool and drowned her. That one, *The Devil of Fever Swamp*, gave her one of the worst head colds she'd ever had. After that, Nick turned apologetic for a while and said this would be the last year, no more short films, but next year, they were at it again, and Gail was out with him in the woods, digging a grave for herself.

She'd pretended then that it drove her crazy, though really it was the highlight of the season for her. And even though Nick had been gone three years now, autumn always came around with a feeling of expectation, like she had a job to do, a role to play. As soon as the leaves starting turning, she felt an impulse to carry out her tasks with grace, no matter what was asked of her.

Nowadays, Gail worked at Oakwood, a mental facility tucked away in the Appalachian foothills. When the nursing director took her on her first tour around the grounds, he told the story about the haunted on-call house and the psychiatrists—reasonable, un-superstitious people, he assured her—who would not stay there overnight. Allegedly, the ghost in the house was that of a patient who had escaped through the air duct seven years ago, stripped off his clothes on his way across the parking lot, and vanished into the kudzu-covered woods on the other side. He drowned himself in the creek just north of the hospital, and the on-call house apparently trapped his desolate ghost and had kept it ever since.

The house itself was a small, plain structure with yellowish siding and a wrap-around porch. A cypress hovered over its east side, a row of boxwoods underneath its windows.

"Folks'll bring pets for company," the nursing director was telling her. "And there's a TV in there, DVD player and everything. Drowns out the noise when the house settles." He laughed. "'Course, most of y'all just stay over on the couches in the lounge. This place is creepy as hell."

Gail was quiet. She had been quiet throughout most of the tour, which caused the nursing director to give her unsure sideways glances, as if he could not see her clearly. He was a grayish, moonfaced man who sought to make others comfortable, the kind of person who liked getting a good read on folks. But Gail had been told that she was more deadpan than most, which was one of the reasons why she had made such good corpses in Nick's horror films. She had few feelings for the nursing director, or for the hospital or its employees or its patients, but she felt *something* when she looked at the on-call house: joy maybe, anticipation, hope.

She settled in for her first overnight visit in October, a month after they took her on as a nurse practitioner at Oakwood, a month after she'd moved out of her mother's house in Cary. She could see the main facility push up through the trees when she approached it from the highway: a stone beast with a spiny gray back. To the east stood a collection of greenhouses where the patients potted plants and grew seedlings, and south of that a garden path encircled a statue of some female Greekish figure overlooking a dry fountain, which had been out of order for years. Alongside the front entrance, they had tacked on a wheelchair ramp.

Gail was a little surprised to find interior of the main facility to be quite modern and clinical, a sea-foam tile floor, wide windows that let in a calm, diffused light, a comfortable nurses' station, each room with spaces and angles that made it look larger than it was. Of course, it was foolish of her to be surprised—this was a still hospital and not a Gothic cathedral, after all—but she couldn't help but feel that the 1980's renovators had smoothed over something profound and theatric.

On the evening of her first stay, Gail stood in a cardigan on the sinking gray porch of the on-call house. She leaned her shoulder against the post at the head of the steps and heard it make a curious sound, like quiet breath. She was listening closely when a bright flash blazed in her periphery.

One of the psychiatric interns, a scruffy guy named Willem, was holding a Polaroid camera just up the walkway.

Gail blinked and squinted at him. "Did you just take my picture?"

Willem looked stunned when she spoke, as though he'd considered her a silent component of the scenery. "Yeah, sorry. I wanted to get some shots of this place and mail them to a couple friends of mine in Kansas City. Oakwood, man. It's ridiculous, you know. You have to see it to believe this place."

"I guess," Gail said. Willem annoyed and intrigued her. When she first saw him in the Women's Wing, a patient came up to him and started speaking about her nightmares as if continuing a conversation that had at one point been

abrupty interrupted. Willem engaged accordingly: "Oh
yeah, girl, that shit is *scary*." He was as lanky as a teenage
boy, his face gentle and smirking, edged with a half-grown
black beard. Striding around in a white coat and corduroys,
his very existence dripped with irony.

"Can I see the picture?" Gail asked.

"Oh, sure, yeah."

Gail fanned the Polaroid until the image began to
reveal itself. It was very blurred, to the point where Gail
looked faceless, but all around were clear shapes, folding
and eddying like a pale lattice that had laid itself over
the image.

"Where did you find this camera?"

"Flea market," he said.

"Of course you did."

Willem laughed. "What's that mean?"

She handed him the photo.

"Oh," Willem said, his brow wrinkling. "Well, that's
weird."

"Something's wrong with your camera," Gail said.

"It's never done that before."

Gail squinted at the picture and laughed. "Ghosts?"

She felt sorry for laughing when she saw that Willem
looked anxious, staring around him at the framework of
the on-call house. Suddenly, Gail felt a full, swarming
sensation that she hadn't noticed before. She pressed her
shoulder against Willem's until the feeling subsided. He
took another picture, and this time it came out normal.

"That is fucked up," Willem said. "This place is fucked
up. Anyone told you yet?"

"Yeah, they told me," Gail said.

"Damn," Willem said. "Well, gotta go. You can hang
on to those pictures."

He started up driveway at a wide-paced saunter. Gail
noticed that his corduroys barely covered his ankles.

"That's it?" she asked. "You don't want to check this out?"

"I'm late, girl," he told her.

Willem was a kid, really, only twenty-five. Gail was

thirty-two. Her mother would tell her he was too immature to be of any interest to Gail, which was probably true, but Gail had not made any friends yet. The Oakwood staff was rather insular and Willem had been the first person to approach her directly.

In the weeks to follow, they didn't talk about the weird phenomenon in the Polaroid, but they did talk about late 90's alternative music and politics and how best to deal with patients who had delusions, versus patients who told lies. Willem annoyed most of the staff, hipster fool that he was, but Gail enjoyed having someone to talk to.

Then it came. He became *interested* in her. Gail felt it on a particular day close to Halloween, when Willem's body language slanted toward her, and his voice softened, and his smirk became warmer. Gail had been steeling her mind for this, had been coaching herself, saying she was ready, saying she wanted. . .

"You want to go to a Halloween party with me?" Willem asked, cornering her in the lounge.

You are in high school, Gail thought. But she agreed.

"I guess. Yeah. That sounds fun."

Gail had worked for seven years at Raleigh General. In this time she got her Master's in nursing and met Nick at one of her classmate's parties. She married him within a year. After Nick died, she quit her job and ended up living with her mother, unemployed, for much longer than she had originally planned. The longer she went without a job, the harder it was to get one, and Oakwood had hardly been at the top of her list. Inevitably, her choice was to be an NP at Oakwood or start at the bottom of the food chain elsewhere as some staff nurse, getting pats on the butt from ancient physicians that the hospital simply wouldn't fire because they had been there so long. As a thirty-two-year-old adult woman, Gail felt she'd earned herself a certain place in the workforce.

She was apprehensive about working at a mental institution, but Gail believed she could make up for this with what her mother used to call "solid, ice-edged competence." She'd always been good at her job. Oakwood was just a different kind of job.

Her mother called every week, anxious as hell about Gail's transition, asking how she felt, asking if she was sure she'd made the right decision. "It's just a chilling thought," she said, "you working at an asylum." Though she knew full well they weren't called asylums anymore. Gail had played with the idea of making up stories about icepick lobotomies and electroshock therapy to mess around with her mother. But after Gail's depression—the three years living at home during her stint of unemployment, the social and professional paralysis—her mother had lost some of her sense of humor.

Conversations typically went like this:

"It's fine. Things are fine here."

"Anything other than fine?" her mother would ask. "You're meeting people?"

"I'm meeting the patients."

"Well, that's not what I mean."

"Yeah. Hey, you know, there's a woman here who's always pregnant. That is, she says she's pregnant. We can't figure out if she's pulling one over on us or if she actually does think she's pregnant. The crazy thing is, her periods have stopped."

"Gail, honey."

"Yeah?"

"Are you engaging with anyone other than crazies?"

"Mom, we don't call them that..."

"I just don't want you to be alone."

Gail refrained from telling her mother about Willem, maybe just out of defiance if nothing else. When you live in your childhood home, jobless, for three years, it's hard not to become something like a teenager again. Gail would be happy to report on her regained self-sufficiency, to tell her mother that she'd received crisis intervention training to defend herself against and restrain, not just patients, but anyone. Anyone who wished her harm. But her mother

wanted to picture Gail dating people, not putting them in
headlocks.

Still, no one could predict how competent she really
was at her Oakwood job. She performed efficient, thorough
physicals—firm, but not unkind. Gail felt as if she'd seen
the vagina of every supposed madwoman in the county.
She'd become skilled at detecting lies too, to be skeptical
when the patients asked specifically for Vicodin, for Oxy.
A rail-thin woman named Lavinia complained about her
pain every day, but she ate like a horse, especially on
pancake Sunday, and she claimed to be allergic to any
medication that, incidentally, did not have codeine in it.

Probably the most important thing Gail learned was
that these women did not need or want anyone's pity. Drug
addicts, agoraphobics, hypochondriacs, builders of sky
castles. These were people who had been abused, indulged,
hated, neglected, but they had acquired their ways because
these were methods that had ensured their survival.
Sometimes they despised Gail and spat at her feet, but
Gail knew she could not despise them back. They were
living. You couldn't fault a person for living.

When Willem showed up at Gail's place to drive her to
the Halloween party, he was wearing an old-fashioned
nurse's uniform, complete with a wig, cap and white
stockings.

"Nurse Ratched," he told her.

Gail, much less clever, was a fortuneteller, piles of rags
and scarves obscuring her shape. "You are terrible," she said.

At the party she clung to him while all his local friends
crushed in. She knew no one, was older than most of them.
She regretted coming, wondered what had made her agree
in the first place. But after a while, Willem seemed to get
tired of the crowd and took her out to the gravel parking
lot behind the apartment building and kissed her. Half-
drunk, Gail realized how much she had missed this intimate
touching, wanting and being wanted.

But when he took her home, she looked at her smeared

face in the side mirror, a painted, ugly version of herself. She felt overwhelmingly sad and guilty, guilt which was blurred and intensified by drinking. Willem had expectations. She didn't think she could meet them.

"Willem," she said.

"Yeah."

"I was married. My husband died three years ago. He flipped his car."

Willem parked in front of her house. He turned to look at her. Sometime at the party, he had removed his cap and wig, but still had on the stockings and stuffed bra. Gail looked at the bra. She felt the universe was laughing at her misery.

"I'm sorry," he said. "If you want to take it slow. . ."

"No, I just wanted to tell you. I'm not looking for anything real serious right now. I just wanted to tell you."

Willem stared. He hiccupped. "You want to talk about it?"

"No," she said. "I'm pretty tired."

She gathered up her things.

"Hey. Do you mind if I borrow your Polaroid?"

"Uh?" Willem said. "Yeah, sure. I used up the film for it though. You gotta buy that stuff online. It's not cheap."

"That's okay."

Willem undid his seatbelt and reached over the headrest. The camera was sitting in the backseat, which was probably where it had been since he first took pictures around the grounds at Oakwood. He handed it to her.

When he drove off, Gail sat down on the steps of her porch, feeling the weight of the camera in her hands. She felt relieved to have the device without Willem attached to it. She felt relieved to watch his taillights recede into the darkness, leaving her on her porch alone.

The weather had turned cold by the time the film for Willem's camera came in. On a particular night in November, Gail set up a space heater in the on-call house and slept with it running. This was the night she felt the ghosts swarm in.

A rare fullness overcame the room, one that only exists
when you are with someone who knows you well, when
you are connected and aware of another person's thoughts
and feelings, and they are aware of yours. Gail felt as
attuned to the crowding ghosts as to her own body. But
perhaps this was what they were, Gail's own body,
multiples of Gail, quantum Gails born every time an atom
decayed and a new universe bubbled up into being. There
existed an infinite number of them, infinite possibilities.

Gail took Willem's Polaroid camera from the bedside
table and snapped a photo of the opposite wall. When the
photo developed, she could see the ghosts inside, trembling
shapes at the edges of the frame, nervous animals. Gail
rose from the bed and snapped more photos throughout
the on-call house, linoleum kitchen and tiny, tiled
bathroom. When the photos developed, the distorted fish-
eyed shapes pushed toward the edges of the frame. She
wanted to understand them, to see them in their entirety.
There was a message here.

She had every light in the house burning when she burst
out the front door, barefoot on the ice-whitened steps. She
snapped her photos into the darkness, up the drive where
the brooding silhouette of the hospital stood.

So many!

But the shapes became thinner and fewer. When her
last photo developed, there was nothing in it but the black
woods and the drive, which glowed pale from the flash.

She took the photos inside and laid them out on the
floor so that she could see them all at once. Maybe that
was where the message was. If she pulled back far enough,
it would reveal itself to her, then it would not be just Gail.
It would be Gail and the ghosts and their secrets.

The following week, she showed Willem the pictures she
had taken.

"What do you know about this stuff?" she asked him.

Willem was less intrigued with the pictures than she
might have thought. He looked at them, fanned out on

the counter of the nurse's station. Then he looked at his ID badge.

"It's not just your camera, either," Gail said, "though they do show up better in the Polaroids. You can see a bit of something with a disposable camera too. They're all over the place. Maybe the drowned man was the first to get trapped here, but there are so many others."

"Gail," Willem said, his voice remonstrative. "Why are you messing with this?"

She stared at Willem's face, which was more sincere than she'd ever seen it. He had shaved off his beard-scruff and was no longer wearing pants that were too short for him.

"The people who work here know about it, don't they?" she asked. "At least, they know about the drowned man."

"Yeah, they know about it," Willem said. "But they don't mess with it. You shouldn't mess with stuff like that. You shouldn't—*look* for stuff like that."

"Why?" Gail asked, laughing. "You think I'll get possessed?"

"No," he said. "Not possessed. Well, maybe. I don't know. I've been here over a year. We just don't mess with it."

"But you know there's something."

"Everyone knows there's something."

His response disappointed and frustrated her. Everyone knew there was something. Surrounding the grounds was a tangible miasma. Deer and rabbits never came into the adjacent fields when they were fallow, and even the grackles wouldn't sit long on the power lines across the road without looking nervous. A service dog someone brought in for a blind patient once sat on the steps and whined and gnawed on its legs. It would not come inside.

On her way back to her car that day, Gail snapped a picture of a blue Pontiac Tempest parked in the drive, which belonged to one of the psychiatrists in the Women's Wing. The car's windows were cracked, and when the photograph developed, Gail could see the ghosts getting in and settling down in the back seat. Everyone knew there was something. Did they know the ghosts followed people home?

◆ ◆ ◆

Gail decided to open the boxes with Nick's things in them. It wasn't like she thought she'd be able to summon him—nothing as specific as that. But if these items could help her understand what she was seeing, it would be worth the physical pain of taking them out and looking at them. Here was his life's work, photography contests submitted to and lost. Here were his books and bad horror movies: *Plan 9 from Outer Space, Blood Diner, Chopping Mall, 976-EVIL*, and his personal favorite, *976-EVIL II: The Astral Factor.* At the bottom of the box she found his glasses, the ones he'd been wearing in the crash, but the lenses were missing.

Next when she stayed over at the on-call house, she placed the box open in a corner of the room. But nothing happened that night. The box was too heavy. Too much. She watched the movies, one after the other, until she fell asleep on the couch.

It was hard to say that the ghosts in the photographs looked like anything. They were, in a sense, formless: at first glance smooth, curved shapes; at second glance, jagged; at third, a series of loops and lines, layered over one another. Gail would hold them to her nose and then pull them back the way she'd done her Magic Eye books when she was a child—stereograms. Let your eyes kind of cross and you can see a dolphin or a heart pop out in 3D from underneath. She thought she saw things, complex things: her mother by the windowsill in her childhood home, circus animals, the blurred runners of her high school track team. Sometimes she saw children, or a child—an amorphous creature with many limbs and eyes and smiles.

She was nervous about showing them to people after what Willem had said, and she certainly wouldn't show the photos to patients.

Once, the unit manager—a gray, wiry woman named Zora—caught her looking at them in the lounge. Zora seemed like the last person to be interested in what was haunting the hospital, but she seemed inquisitive when she looked over Gail's shoulder.

"Workin' hard?" she asked.

"No," Gail said. She waved one of the pictures in front of Zora's nose. "You've been here a long time. You must know about this as well as anybody. What do you see?"

Zora took the picture and squinted through her glasses. "Looks like psoriasis."

"No, pull it back from your nose. Let your eyes cross."

Zora glanced at Gail, but she obeyed, her expression focusing and not focusing at the same time. "Looks like a man. Short man. Bald. Big, egg yolk eyes." She returned the photograph to Gail. "My ex-husband, the bastard. It's a dead ringer for him—but he's been in the ground seven years now."

Gail stacked the Polaroids together. "That's very specific," she said. She wasn't sure if she felt envious or disappointed.

Zora looked like she was about to launch into an assertion, possibly a reprimand, but then Willem appeared in the lounge doorway with a clipboard in his arm.

"Code Grey downstairs, ladies."

Zora looked offended. "Why the hell didn't they call it? What's wrong with the intercom?"

Willem raised his eyebrows but didn't answer. He disappeared down the hall. In his absence, Zora clicked her tongue.

"I liked him better when he was an intern," she said. "He acted like a sixteen-year-old at a drama camp, but at least he wasn't a pompous ass."

So, Gail thought, Willem was a resident now. Dr. Willem—how absurd that was. Dr. Willem buying flea market junk like an Asheville hippie, dressing in drag at Halloween parties. He was different now, she guessed, but when had his change taken place? It seemed like only last week that Willem had begun shaving like an adult person, and just a week or so before that they'd kissed in the parking lot behind his friend's apartment building.

"Zora," Gail said, "how long have I been working here?"
Zora tilted her head and counted to herself. After a
while, she gave up. "Hell, time does blur together in this
place. I can't safely say how long *I've* been working here,
let alone you. Who knows anything about you? You
don't speak."

"I speak," Gail said. This accusation astonished Gail.
She had not been actively cutting herself off from the rest
of the nursing staff, but they were cliquey, girly, most of
them married, many of them with children. Sometimes one
of them would be crying in the lounge because a patient
had called her a name, and the rest would hover around in
there and comfort her. What was Gail supposed to do? Reach
her hand into the huddle, a relative stranger, and say, "There,
there"? Yes, she admitted, part of the reason why she hadn't
worked her way into the huddle was because she didn't
have the energy. She'd resolved herself to the belief that she
would never again have the comfortable group of friends
she'd had at Raleigh General. Now, during the birthday
things and the mini-celebrations—someone was getting
married, someone was having a baby—Gail watched from
afar as the women showered love and attention on one
another.

Of course, when you live in your childhood home,
jobless, for three years, it's easy to forget how to make
small talk. The friends from Raleigh General had kept in
touch as well as anyone could, but it was hard under those
circumstances. It was sad and humiliating and hard.

She'd never intended to quit work after Nick died; in
fact, she went back three weeks after the funeral, an attempt
to restore balance to her life. To stop working would be to
turn brittle, to collapse, so she filled up her schedule—
worked in the day and took night shifts, went out with
friends in between. Friends encouraged her to drink, to
take up smoking. A little self-destructive behavior after
something like this is perfectly common, expected even.
Everyone commended her bravery.

But then she woke up cramping. She took a Midol and

went on to work, but the cramps intensified, and by noon she was bleeding, and stars were bursting in front of her eyes whenever she stood up. She began to disconnect from her body. She wandered in a haze until someone stopped her and told her she was bleeding through her scrubs.

At no point had she realized she was pregnant, and no one could say that anything specific she'd done had caused the miscarriage. Gail had already had two miscarriages, one before they were married and one afterward, so she and Nick hadn't been actively trying to have children. She'd even conceded that she and Nick would've made for immature parents, Nick especially. He liked to be waited on. When he had a cold, he was worthless, sniffling and moping to elicit her pity, asking her to rub his chest with Vicks VapoRub, asking her to make him peppermint tea.

Still, it was as if he'd died twice. One death was a strident echo of the other. One possibility, two possibilities—both collapsing and bursting, insidious might-have-beens that would never leave her. She'd hated Nick and his miscarried child for handing her this. What could she make from it? Where could she possibly go from here?

Time progressed, but it seemed as if Oakwood never moved beyond autumn. The weather was always chilly, and the naked trees never budded green the way they did in the rest of the world. When Gail laid out the photographs on the floor of the on-call house, the color pallet was always rich red-brown and yellow, scattered with silvery specters.

She'd moved much of her stuff into the on-call house. Nobody ever used it, so she would stay there for weeks at a time cooking her dinners in the little yellow kitchen, showering and dressing while the house settled around her. Those creepy sounds had become familiar. It had crossed her mind to cancel her lease altogether, but she couldn't bring herself to do it. Living at the mental institution for good had connotations, no matter how well she did her job.

Willem had begun fading to a memory when the staff started saying that he and one of the nursing technicians were dating. Then they were engaged. Then in an eye-blink, the girl was pregnant. Gail overheard two nurses carrying on about it in the hallway while she was interviewing one of her patients.

"Remember him when he first came here? Such a baby!"

"Oh, I couldn't stand him. You'd have thought this place was a playground the way he chased tail, but he's grown into himself, I think. He'll be sweet to her."

Gail listened half to the nurses and half to her patient. When she realized she'd written something down wrong, she went to the doorway.

"You two are being loud," she said.

The nurses looked up.

"Did you hear Dr. Prier is getting married?" one asked.

Gail's patient scooted to the edge of her seat and leaned forward. She was large but not fat, her face hawkish, somewhat ravaged. "Who's getting married?" she demanded.

"Please," Gail said to the nurses. "Please, *him*? He is a child. Him and his shotgun wedding, he hasn't grown into anything."

The nurses looked unhappy about this accusation. One of them counted on her fingers. "But they've been engaged for—"

"Whatever," Gail said. "Just, whatever. I hope it works out for him. But I'm just saying, the math doesn't lie, does it."

"I had a baby out of wedlock," Gail's patient said. "You want to come back to your little desk and judge me for it? At least they're *gettin'* married. My man hitchhiked cross-country to get away from me. What you got to say to that?"

This uncomfortable moment probably lasted much longer in Gail's mind than it did in reality. She felt strange and terrible anger rising in her, but she couldn't unleash it on the two nurses, and she certainly couldn't unleash it on the patient. She remembered Willem's camera, sitting on the dresser in the on-call house and imagined herself fending him off if he showed up on the front porch to get it back. She imagined herself lapsing into a childish tantrum. No, I'm still using it! I still need it! She had learned nothing and everything, and there was more to see.

But he never came for the camera, never even asked about it.

Afterward, it seemed as though Gail's comment about Willem's marriage, which she knew was mean-spirited, had gotten her a bad rapport. The staff rallied around Dr. Prier and his new wife and sent them off warmly on their honeymoon. Gail stood to the side, still the taciturn NP who took pictures of the ghosts. She was caught up, self-absorbed. She stopped answering her mother's phone calls, and eventually her mother called up reception in hysterics, begging someone to let her speak to her daughter.

"I called you six times," her mother said.

"I know. I'm sorry I didn't answer. I've been busy."

"Has something happened? Were you attacked by a patient?"

"No. Nothing's happened."

"Why didn't you call me back?"

Gail sat thinking about this. She had not called back because the conversations were always the same. There was nothing she could say to her mother and nothing her mother could say to her that would shed new light on any problems or events or issues. There was nothing enjoyable about the conversations—they pained her mother, she could tell, and to have this pain come at her via cellular satellite, knowing that it had flown up into space only to be bounced back to this miserable stony planet once again, was intolerable.

"Honey," her mother said after a long silence. "I just— sometimes I can't stand thinking of you out there by yourself. Sometimes I just wish you'd come back here and stay near me."

"No!" Gail shouted, horrified. A couple of psychiatrists looked at her from across the lobby. Eyeing them, she hung up the phone slowly.

◆ ◆ ◆

Gail bought more film, took more pictures. She littered the floor of the on-call house with them, but while she searched for balance, the universe around her shifted. She didn't find out that Willem had landed a new job in Atlanta until she saw it posted on the events bulletin. She overheard from someone else that his wife had already been accepted into a Master's program there. They were leaving Oakwood behind.

Since he'd clearly forgotten about the Polaroid, she didn't feel bad keeping it, but she had made no progress in figuring out the true nature of the ghosts. They were as elusive to her as ever, sometimes nearly decipherable and fully formed, sometimes smears of white with no message, no answer at all. Outside, the leaves had become crystalized in ice, clinking against each other when the wind blew. Gail fell asleep listening to their dissonant music. Snow fell, melted, and froze again.

It was on a night like this that the drowned man appeared to her. No more hidden by a trellis of blurs or fuzzy lines, no more a secret shape to discover. Fighting off sleep, Gail propped herself up on her elbows and saw him nude at the foot of her bed, lazy-eyed, his lips blue and swollen. He was so old, so badly aged he seemed mummified. The crown of his head was bald, with whitish fuzz around his ears. He seemed to shrink when she looked at him, his body stretched and ravaged by the current of the icy stream in which he'd drowned.

"It's you," Gail said.

The ghost opened his mouth as if to speak, but it was stuffed full of leaves and mud and acorns. Gail shuddered.

"Say something," she said. "Tell me something."

But it was clear he couldn't speak.

Silence. The ghosts were silent. They had no message. She could feel them now, working to swamp and submerge her body with their emptiness. A sound came to her, like a sigh, breath leaving a body, and the room went suddenly cold. She shivered, became terrified. Get out of the house.

Get out of the house or freeze, be stuck forever. So she tore the covers from her body and tried to gather up her husband's things in their box, to save them from whatever was overtaking her, them. In her frenzy, she rammed her knee into the corner of the dresser and heard Willem's camera hit the floor. A piece of it broke off and clattered away into the dark.

All the while, the drowned man stood where he had appeared at the foot of the bed. He watched her with his dead, mute expression, and he was watching her still as she fled, limping, out of the house.

When she reached the gravel drive, the porch collapsed behind her.

Gail stood very still, barefoot on a thin sheet of wet snow. From where she stood, she could see the rot that had been working its way deep into the posts. Beneath the eaves, the wood was almost black, shingles hanging limp as paper.

The sound of the crashing porch brought some on-call folks out from the main facility. They looked at the house and looked at Gail. Nurse Zora came up, squinting in the dark.

"What happened?" she asked. "Are you hurt?"

Gail couldn't tell her. She wasn't sure of anything.

Nurse Zora whipped her head around. "Wait a minute—you're not on call tonight. What are you doing here?"

"Nurse Jamison, she's been basically *living* here," someone said.

Gail shook beneath their stares. Her feet ached from cold and her knee stung, bleeding through the leg of her pajamas "My things," she whispered, pointing to the ruined porch. "I have to—go back in—get my things. Can someone help me?"

Sometime later, Gail was sitting in a car outside of Willem's house. It was a nice house, and she watched as movers came and wrapped up pieces of avant-garde art, the kind that hangs in coffee houses, so that they could pack it away in a white van. Willem's wife was a short, temperamental-looking girl. She moved in and out of the front door, fully dressed but in slippers.

Gail held the camera in her lap. Though she was sure it was beyond repair, she felt an impulse to return it to its original owner. She waited for the right moment to approach, considered if there was in fact a right moment to approach at all. When Willem came out into view, the sharp, afternoon light made him look so much older than she remembered. His hair had begun to recede, and he'd put on a little bit of weight in his face. How strange to see Willem outside of Oakwood, in a neighborhood so pristinely different from that place's dim, gothic flavor. And then, as she watched, two children followed him out into the yard. Two, dark-haired girls—his oldest now looking about five, his youngest a toddler.

Gail regarded the children with a strange sensation. She didn't dislike them, but they were alien to her, as bizarre as if they had grown from fruit trees overnight. They grow so fast.

A jogger ran by Gail's passenger window. A man came out to get his newspaper, shaking it when he found it wet with melted snow. But Gail sat there still. Even when the sky grew dark, when Willem and his family had long since gone inside, even then, she sat still, moving only to place her hand over the stack of photographs in her pocket.

Castle Links Creek

In September of '99, I remember the hurricane that flooded our town, twenty square miles of farms and lowlands already saturated in rainfall. The trailer parks along Highway 40, where my best friend Christine lived, that was a mess, water pale like coffee creamer, all the way up to the windowsills, whole neighborhoods like that. So while Christine's mom and uncle worked things out with the aid workers, Christine stayed at my house in the suburbs.

My parents occupied themselves cutting and moving the fallen oak trees in our backyard, so they left Christine and me to our own devices. It was hard to keep her entertained. She stayed up later, woke up earlier than I did, and when the power came back on in the night, she told me the news stories I'd missed out on by falling asleep. Some service worker died when her car got swept off the road. They found it half-sunk in a reservoir nearby, roof clawed up, the dead woman's French manicure worn to nubs.

The hurricane had killed people in the area, sure, but, as with most things Christine, I didn't know if this particular story was true or if she'd invented it. This was back in the eighth grade when a lie wasn't just to hurt someone, or to keep someone from getting hurt. A lie could be like a tart fruit, something you'd hold in your mouth. We could pretend belief in a story we knew wasn't true, if only to explore its flavor.

But as I said, Christine was restless at my place, and on the third day following the hurricane, she woke me up from bed, mud and leaves pasted to her ankles, morning breath sour against my ear. At first, I didn't hear what she was saying, still stuck in a clumsy haze of sleep. The sun hadn't risen yet, and the room was filled with bluish, pre-dawn light. My parents probably weren't even up.

Christine spoke louder, enunciating sharply "I need. To take you. To the Pittards' house. I found a *grave*."

That's right. Lies. Rumors. We were big on rumors, and one of them had to do with Marybeth Pittard, a girl in our grade at the middle school, and a dead baby. The Pittards' house was only a half-mile from mine, in a subdivision a little newer, a little more expensive. You could take a shortcut there if you followed Castle Links Creek, which snaked all the way up to the golf course on the north side of the subdivision. A stretch of woods flanked the creek on both sides—mossy oaks and brambly underbrush cutting through our neighborhood like a spine, this being the dangerous path Christine said she'd taken. I told her no at first, said I wasn't interested in Marybeth Pittard anymore, didn't care about her dead baby, but Christine climbed atop my shoulders and shook me—"Get—your—fat—ass—up"—mud everywhere, all over the duvet, and I gave in.

A few minutes later, we were moving along the milky, swollen creek. The sky was a little lighter now, filled with dull, yellowish clouds, but it was still just dark enough to make the woods seem like a cave around us. The air smelled damp, weirdly electric in the primal, post-apocalyptic mood of the after-storm, as if the hurricane had shed us of civilization. We hiked our way along the bank, barefoot, grabbing each other's hands when we stumbled. In time, we began to take drunken pleasure in each other's company,

the way we usually did on expeditions like these. I saw
Christine keeping an anticipatory eye on the black debris
in the water. Her brain was working, perhaps elaborating
silently on the mythos of Marybeth Pittard and her baby. I
hoped so, because I'd lied; I was still interested. I would be
interested as long as Christine was. But Christine didn't
mention Marybeth, not yet.

"Did you know that crocodiles let the British win World
War II?" she asked me.

"No. I thought *we* won World War II."

"We won and the British won. Have you ever heard of
the Ramree Massacre?"

I said I hadn't.

"Ramree's an island. Somewhere in Asia—India, I think.
So in World War II, the British were fighting the Japanese.
They got them all surrounded and forced them into the
mangrove swamp. Then in the night, the British hear
screaming, crazy screaming." She looked at me, seemed to
be holding her breath. "It was crocodiles."

We paused, listening to the dull rush of the creek,
yearning, perhaps, to also hear the shrieks of the Japanese
soldiers in the mangroves. I contemplated the likelihood
of crocodiles in my suburb, giving it a seriousness of
thought I hadn't given the warnings of my parents. Things
were dangerous right now, they'd said, with all the downed
power lines and the sewage that had flushed out from the
turkey farm to the north, though the day after the storm,
Christine and I had been right out in the middle of it,
searching around the neighborhood for wreckage to
investigate. The creek itself, suffused with toxic run-off
on a good day, ran with a wild current that could probably
have drowned us like rats.

"Crocodiles," Christine said. "The swamps were crawling
with them. In the night, the British heard them spinning in
the water. That's how they tear the meat from their prey, by
spinning. One thousand Japanese soldiers went into the
swamp. In the morning there were twenty left."

"Motherfucking crocodiles," I said.

"Motherfucking crocodiles!" said Christine, louder, and soon we were screaming it, out-screaming each other, our voices echoing off the trees and the houses just beyond. MOTHERFUCKING CROCODILES! We erupted with laughter; an observer wouldn't have been able to make sense of our hysterics. Crocodiles suddenly seemed the appropriate monster for any occasion, and I began to weave a scenario in which the good-natured reptiles laid siege to the neighborhood pools. All those snobby bitches who live out here, floating lazy-like on their rafts, blond hair stiff with lemon juice—MOTHERFUCKING CROCODILES! And I clamped my arms like jaws around Christine's waist. She grinned and stage-screamed and pretended I was eating her. Then her laughter tapered off and she said, "Okay, okay. Let's chill out. We're on a mission here."

She untangled herself from my arms and moved a little quicker, and I watched her dark head bob as she pulled herself over a mound of collapsed branches. She had done up her hair in characteristic style: two slick knots on the top of her head ("Giraffe horns," my mother had mockingly called them). She wore studded leather bracelets, hand-me-down metal band T-shirts of her brother's; to me, who didn't know any better, she was a genuine punk. My parents didn't like her. They felt sorry for her and her family in the wake of the storm, but they didn't like her. Most people didn't.

I watched her bobbing head, her giraffe horns. We maneuvered our way through a tangle of briars, the thorns sticking in our skin, and I said, "So you were serious about walking all the way to the Pittards' house this morning. By yourself."

"What else did I have to do?" she asked, and there was an edge to the question. I lowered my voice, an attempt to quiet a series of miring doubts.

"And you found a grave."

"Yeah. I found a grave. I found the baby's grave."

Even if I didn't entirely believe Christine, I could still

trust her. I was willing to brave the creek, to trespass on the Pittard's property and see what she had found.

I should make a few more things clear about Marybeth Pittard. She was not our friend. She hadn't liked me since fifth grade, when her family hosted the end-of-year picnic for our class and I spooked her horses by setting off a firecracker one of the boys had brought. Boys were my closest friends prior to middle school, but then a geological shift engaged, and they turned indifferent, and then cruel. Overnight, it seems, I doubled in size, became a chubby, flat-chested, pasty-skinned pear, too chickenshit to set off a firecracker now and too ugly to be of interest otherwise. And Christine—well, she had always been ugly, chinless, sallow, with prominent eyeteeth. She was what the kids called White Trash, and when I glued myself to her, I became TBA, Trash By Association. I felt lucky. Christine encouraged disdain toward boys and the hatred of girly girls like Marybeth. Girls who seemed immune to the crushing awkwardness and uncomfortable smells that accompanied puberty.

There was another thing. Marybeth's friends were all white girls, various shades of tan and golden and various levels of pretty, though Marybeth herself was not a white girl; the Pittards had adopted her from India as a baby. There wasn't much to distinguish Marybeth from the white girls—she wore the same brand-named clothes, talked in the same bored tones with sentences that ended like questions. She played volleyball. She liked chicken biscuits. But she struck in Christine a specific kind of resentment.

"You know I'm not racist," she had told me, "but it pisses me off how someone gets to be popular just because they're, like, exotic. Before the Civil War, my great-great-grandparents *owned* half this state. Her parents were—what—rice farmers? *Bull*shit."

Sure, I'd said. Bullshit. Though I knew the fixation didn't make much sense. It was not as if Marybeth had stolen a spot that Christine or I would otherwise have, and in the spring of last year, when Christine's attitude changed, I remember being surprised at how quickly resentment transitioned to morbid fascination. We heard about it toward the end of summer, that Marybeth had gotten pregnant by one of the high school boys, that she'd had an abortion sometime in April. In late July, I recall Christine and me hanging around in the vacant lot behind the Piggly Wiggly, and Larissa Mitchell stopped by in her four-wheeler and told us about it, about the guy, Todd.

"We don't know a Todd," I said. "We don't care to know a Todd."

"No?" said Larissa, mildly surprised, as if we'd admitted a sad shortcoming.

Christine and I shook our heads.

"It's Todd. Trust me. I heard—come here, listen," she lowered her voice to a whisper, though no one was listening, "my sister said Todd's family paid Marybeth's parents like a million dollars for it."

"For what?" asked Christine.

"For—for *it*, you know, to get rid of it!" Larissa's cheeks flushed. "Jesus, it's hot. What are you dumbasses *doing* out here?"

"Digging holes," Christine said.

"The Green County Strangler buried his victims out here," I said.

Larissa looked as us with wonder. "You guys are so lame. This is why no one likes you."

It was probably also Larissa who told us it was state law that abortion doctors had to give you the fetus so you could bury it—they'd get arrested if they didn't. Maybe we believed this and maybe we thought she was full of shit, but regardless, Christine began to fixate on the fetus. And I thought it odd at the time, because she didn't disparage Marybeth for the sex or for the abortion, which some kids certainly did. No, Christine didn't judge her. She *mined* her. She formed the belief early on that the Pittards had buried Marybeth's baby in their backyard. She had drawn pictures of what it probably looked like at the time of its burial—all lizard-like and bug-eyed, with its bumpy vestigial tail—and she told me this was a creature she'd seen in her dreams. In the space of Christine's imagination, which by extension had become mine, Marybeth's baby, both real and not real, formed and half-formed, began to take on the shape of a hideous ghost, which Christine said she suspected was haunting her. "Nothing in the world is harder to exorcise than the spirit of an unborn baby"—such was a rule of Christine's invention—"They're *relentless.*" But why her? Why Christine specifically? When I asked this, Christine changed her story. She suspected the baby was in fact haunting everyone in town, that she'd felt a change in the adults since we heard the news. She was connected to all this simply by virtue of a supernatural intuition she claimed to have, which skipped generations in her family.

So that's why we were headed there, to the Pittards' backyard, and I was recalling the Ouija board nights and the binding spells we cast against people we hated, Christine's forays into witchcraft. I believed her, I did, when she said she was haunted, or at least, I believed she was haunted by something. The sun began to rise, and with it I assumed I would feel renewed trust in her adventurous spirit. However, as the colors brightened around us, the shapes and shadows of the broken trees composed frightening angles, and the sound of the creek seemed to grow louder. Its turbulent waters had gone from gray to a strange, chemical orange. Black mud, thick and shiny, sucked at our feet. We should have at least worn shoes.

I was falling behind—Christine was nimbler than me—and I was starting to get irritated with her, and irritated with myself for being afraid. Further on, we came across a wooden frame covered with slats of corrugated tin, part of a roof maybe that the creek had violently thrown across the bank. Christine climbed up on top of it.

"This creek is running faster than I thought," I said, trying to sound as if I were familiar with the creek and its various moods. "I think we should head back."

She didn't answer me. She was sliding her bare foot along the tin.

"This is cool. We could drag this back and use it to rebuild your tree house."

"Didn't you see this earlier?" I asked.

Christine gave me a quick look and then said no, it must have washed up recently. She crouched down and ran her finger along a row of exposed nails. "Watch your feet. You'll get tetanus."

"I don't think you were here earlier," I said.

Christine glared at me over her shoulder, stood straight, and hopped down. As she did, her weight shifted one of the tin slats, and its movement sent her off balance. I screamed and reached for her arm, but she fell away from me and landed on her hands and knees with a *pluk*, half submerged in the muddy bank. By the time I had made my way around the obstruction, Christine was laughing. I crouched down next to her.

"Was that graceful or what?" she said.

"You weren't out here before. You said you came out here earlier this morning, and there's no way. It would've been too dark to see anything."

She frowned at me, stood and kept going, smearing her muddy hands on her shorts. I saw she had a bleeding cut on her leg, though I wasn't sure how it had gotten there.

"Chris-*tine*," I said.

"I still know the grave's there," she told me.

"But you don't *know*. Why do you keep telling these stories?"

"You don't get it," she said. In her spooky blue eyes, I saw mysticism and power, both of which I envied and admired. "It was a dream. I had a dream about it. In the dream, I was Marybeth, and I was running around the track at school. Then I take this turn past the gym, and suddenly I'm in the Pittards'—in *my*—backyard. And there's this little kind of Stonehenge place there, and in the center of the stones, there this one white stone with blood on it, like a

cross. And I knew. In the dream, I knew that's where I—
she—buried the baby. So I just *know*, okay?"

Christine took in a deep breath and wiped a spot of
mud off her forehead.

"Either way, I have to go there to see."

I shifted uneasily, glancing behind us at the black-brown
tangle of woods. "But—"

"If you don't believe me, you can go back home and
I'll go on by myself."

You could not dispute dreams. If Christine said she
dreamed a vision and was sure it meant something, I
couldn't say she hadn't and it didn't, nor could I counter
her with a dream of my own that said there wasn't a grave
at the Pittard's house. This would break an unsaid rule.

"But we *hate* Marybeth Pittard," I said finally. "I don't
get why we have to care so much about her stupid baby.
It's not like it's *your* baby."

"Go on back then," said Christine, and then, with a bit
of venom: "I can't just sit around at *your* place all day."

She continued on, and when she turned away from me,
I felt the usual ice water chill that accompanied
disappointing her. Doubting Christine's stories hurt,
because part of me knew she was wiser than me, because
I too had admitted to feeling haunted.

"Do you think maybe it's the town?" I asked the back
of her head, my voice coming out in a rush. "Because the
town's been weird since this happened, and we haven't
seen Marybeth out?"

"I don't care about this stupid hick town," Christine said.

I pressed on. "I'm just trying to think of explanations
for what we're feeling, because you know this has been on
everyone's mind, and they don't talk about it. Like—maybe
they know something they aren't telling us."

She didn't answer. I couldn't see her face, so I couldn't
tell if she was still angry.

The smell of manure signaled that we were approaching
the Pittard's property line. A few minutes more, still
following the creek, we emerged from the woods into a

cool green space of manicured lawn. The Pittards had lost
trees, several small oaks and poplars. Their tool shed leaned
to one side and was missing half its roof, and I realized
this was probably what we'd found on the bank a ways
back. Otherwise, the chaos seemed managed. Their house
stood untouched, a patchwork of brick and white siding
at the head of the slope. It was a relief to be out of the
woods, but the sudden exposure put me on edge, made
me crouch like a buzzard. Christine paused, craning her
neck toward the house.

"Lights are off," she said. "Is the power still out over here?"

"Maybe," I whispered.

The creek carried on to our left. A long dark shape
moved with the current, and my mind grew suddenly rich
with images of crocodiles.

"Motherfucking crocodiles," I offered.

"Quit it," said Christine. "That joke's old now."

She stood at the edge of the yard. There was no one we
could see to stop us, but she hesitated, as if she had expected
there would be, as if she had imagined our journey up
until this moment and no further. I realized later, but not
then, that this was the error in her story. We could prove
or disprove the existence of a grave at the Pittards' house,
and now there was no choice but to look for one.

"Okay," Christine said. "Okay." She picked up a stick
and began searching through a thicket of azaleas and
blackberry bushes, and I followed her example, the Pittards'
alien-green lawn bright against our muddy feet, which were
scraped and cut from the journey. We were little gremlins,
scrabbling in the brush, and with each prick of the
blackberry thorns, I sensed the heat of my own frustration.
Of course there would be nothing. She knew, I knew, we
would find nothing, and for all the danger we'd put ourselves
in, that I had put myself in for her sake. . .

But there *was* something. When I moved around to the
other side of the thicket, closer to the house, I did find
something.

There, half-hidden in the grass, was a flat white stone

the size of a notebook. I gazed at it, stunned. It was simple, no inscription, weathered, but roughly square. At this time, an indistinct voice came to me from up toward the house, and I jumped back, scanning wildly for a place to hide. It made no difference. I was already seen. As I turned around, I realized what Christine and I had missed—the Pittards' barn with part of its roof caved in, shattered bits of white-painted wood strewn all across the pasture. Marybeth was watching me, her hands gripping the wire fence that surrounded the field.

"What are you doing here?" she asked.

Her eyes were red, purple shadows underneath them, wetness on her cheeks. She had been crying. Though her face was as sleepy and pretty as I remembered it, she seemed coarser somehow, cheeks acned and hardened. She'd pinned me but hadn't noticed Christine, hiding on the other side of the thicket. I waited, perhaps thinking Christine would give me whispered instructions. Silence.

I was aware of my monster-ness, a cretin-of-the-swamp covered in mud and leafy debris. Slugs crawled on my windbreaker. My hair was in my face. I surveyed the green pasture and the barn and Marybeth judging and staring, and I realized I could see no horses.

"Where are your horses?" I asked.

"They died," she said.

"All of them?"

"All but one. Look, what are you *doing* here?"

I heard a small movement in the thicket behind me, but Marybeth, I think, did not. In truth, I felt bad about the horses, and I felt bad for trespassing, and for what I'd seen under the blackberry bush. But I was angry at having been caught, at Christine's nimble form hiding in silence on the other side of the thicket. The stone was a wondrous find, but it made a looming, disheartening shadow.

With Marybeth's eyes blazing against my face, I felt my cheeks and neck flush with heat. I knew I needed to say something. So it was: "Sorry about the horses. If it makes you feel better, Christine's family lost their trailer."

I heard a sharp hiss from behind the thicket, the angry stab of air through teeth. Marybeth lifted her chin and looked past me, wrinkled her nose in disgust.

"Is someone else here? Who is that? Is that Christine Grubb?"

"No," I said.

"Look, when my daddy gets back, he'll shoot y'all."

That was when I heard Christine taking off behind me, her feet slapping against the wet ground. I turned and ran after her, and I wouldn't see Marybeth until she returned to high school junior year, and she would never ask me about that time Christine and I showed up in her backyard, or, to my knowledge, mention it to anyone else. It must have seemed sad, the way Christine ran off and left me. All along the creek, I stumbled to catch up with her, crashing through the mud, grabbing at the trees, which scraped my palms, shouting at her to stop, I had something to tell her, stop. The creek raged, its watery rush echoing off the wet leaves and branches, and for a moment, I thought she couldn't hear me. The words were in my throat, rising, willing to burst out if she would slow down and wait for me—"I saw it! You were right, Christine! I saw it!"—but she looked over her shoulder and kept going, and I didn't say these words. Soon she had disappeared from my sight, left me struggling along on the bank, unsticking my feet from the mud. A tendril of briars lashed across my face with such pain that it brought me to a halt. I slumped down by the creek, felt a brief, irrational panic. If Christine left me in the woods, I'd get lost. I'd die out here without her. But I remembered. I calmed myself and remembered, with a spasm of sudden knowing and strange guilt: I could not get lost in my own neighborhood. Everywhere I looked, I could see houses through the trees. It was just a straight shot from Marybeth's place to mine.

We Are Meant for Greater Things

This girl, she's one of those people you hear about nowadays, living her life for the second time around. She's a slack-faced, dream-eyed sister, born—twice now—at the end of a gravel road outside town, a stone's throw from the slaughterhouse. She abides with a skittish mother and two large black boxer dogs, and she knows that one of the three will die suffering from a snakebite, hopes she can stop it when the time comes, but she doesn't know when it's supposed go down, or if it's still supposed to go down at all. The girl is Birdy. Birdy Brightlane. Sunny name for such a sad body.

But I don't judge her, it's part of the job not to judge her. You'd be sad too, is what I tell myself, after fifteen years at the institution, and besides, these are often sad people, the ones on their second time around. The agency, they call my visits "conversations" to make them sound less clinical, list them on the paperwork informal-like—Convo #1, Convo #2—but Birdy knows what they are. When I come to see her, we sit together on the mossy deck off the back of her mother's house, and we drink strong coffee and I offer her cigarettes, but she declines. She knows I am not her friend.

I used to smoke, she says.

When was this? I ask.

Sometime—she pauses to think a minute. Sometime a while ago. I must have smoked. I remember it.

I can see in her big mooneyes that she's drifting off, and sometimes I try to net her in with questions (Birdy, why don't you stay here, in the now?). But there she goes, which is to say, she's dreaming about what it was like the first time, when she didn't end up here with her mother, at the end of the gravel road outside town, a stone's throw from the slaughterhouse.

She remembers a long drive, she and the man in the fire. She drives; he lights her cigarettes. A cigarette slips, drops down between her thighs. She curses, pulls over, and then, as she's rubbing spit on the burn, they see a peppery cloud mushrooming from an overpass, spilling out into the twilight—a colony of Mexican free-tailed bats. *Tadarida brasiliensis*, she tells me. In college, she wrote a paper about the way their migration patterns affect peach crops. That time? No, both times. Both times she wrote a paper on bats and peach trees, but that time, the first time, she and the man in the fire sat on the hood of the car and watched until they could no longer see, could only hear the tinny *week week week* and the beating of batwings in the darkness. Birdy tells me that's when he said he wanted to marry her, his words all warm and honeyed. That's happenstance (or is it happiness?): a dropped cigarette and some bats and a confession of love.

Birdy and people like her, they're a phenomenon that hasn't gone unnoticed. Physicists have said their piece, a big dump of Scandinavian names popping up on your newsfeed, airy blond whitecoats with the noble brains required to comprehend the paradoxes of time and probability. They wonder if folks like Birdy are proof of the oscillating universe, the Big Bang that starts it off, the Bounce that revs it back up again, over and over. They've given silly names to what Birdy's experiencing: the quantum foam memory sequence, anachronistic recollection, kairotic displacement disorder. From the Greek, *kairos*, Birdy tells me, (she minored in Classics, both times), meaning "the supreme moment." From where I stand, in the muck, among laypeople, it's hard to know whether Birdy is holding on to a lifelong delusion, or if she is actually visualizing the existence of an alternative world, where things turned out better. I have tested her before (even though I'm told not to, that's not my job). I ask about presidents, Superbowl winners, natural disasters—What's in store for us, Birdy? What'll happen in the future? But Birdy looks at me like she doesn't understand the question.

How would *I* know those things, she says.

But don't you remember?

She shakes her head. Her lips are dry, skin flaking like a sugar glaze.

And let's think about the snakebite a minute. You can't remember if it's, if it's the dog or—or your mother who dies.

Birdy's face crumples with guilt. At the kitchen window, the curtains flutter: her mother, watching us. She seems like a very careful woman, not unkind, though I have the sense that she's afraid of her daughter.

I've tried, Birdy says. I mean, I've tried to remember where I was, the first time, when I heard about it. I was with him. I must've been with him, with the children. I guess—you know—that's why I took part in the experiment, because I wanted to remember—*more*.

I know she is ashamed of her obsession with the man in the fire. It's a quality almost universal to her kind, as if memory were a pane of shattered glass. Certain shards, particular ones, they shine their light in your eyes. Because as a teenager, she did remember getting the scholarship for State (though she wonders now if she applied for it only because she knew she had gotten it before). She remembered a series of unexciting boyfriends, which she avoided, a lewd professor, whose class she took with caution, an internship in Savannah, which moved her out of her mother's house.

She bought the car she remembered buying from before, an ancient junker that would break down the following summer (it did), when she'd find herself stranded at a backcountry crossroads on the hottest day of the year (it was). Here, by happenstance, she remembered hitching a ride back home with the man in the fire.

And all this happened the way you remembered it? I ask.

Up to the point, Birdy says, where the man wasn't there.

We sip our coffee in sync. The face of Birdy's mother is a ghost in the window.

When'd all this start, the memories? I ask.

Birdy sits for a minute, working a loose thread on the edge of her sleeve. I'll show you, she says, and she disappears into the shadows of the house, returns with a stack of old journals from her high school years. They are filled with drawings, cartoonish renderings of the man in the fire and their children, two girls, one tanned, one fair, their house with the wrap-around porch, backyard view of the Yadkin River, a tuxedo cat named Sadie or Sasha, she can't recall now, and a peach tree. *Prunus persica*, she tells me. It has always been a peach tree. She talks about how at night (both times) the slaughterhouse stench used to lie on her like a blanket, pig shit and blood, and her body (this time) would ache with hope and joy at the road ahead, and she would think, she would KNOW (this time): *I'm meant for more than all this.*

Birdy's always been a troubled sleeper. The weight of time keeps her awake. She tells me she thought about suicide during her stay at the institution, that she figured her life as a trial run. Maybe the gods, whoever they are (and she's sure they're getting a good long laugh at all this), would send her back around again to get it right.

But that's enough to make a body ill, isn't it. I end up driving home from Birdy's to my cheap, tiny apartment in Corporate Village, all those thoughts flitting like wasps in my head: maybe the Hindus got it right with reincarnation, except for the part about how no other lump of meat would dare have a sister like you, that nothing exists prior to your birth or following your death. Just poor sad *you*, as *you*, as *you*, over and over again on the dented-up disc of time.

I think Birdy was okay until the experiment. After a year, they suspended her internship program because of funding problems (which happened last time), and toward the end (this time) she had a pitiful fling with some fool who gave her an infection, spent time in the hospital, whittled down her savings in copays. Then she found herself picking through a meager pile of shit jobs, clerks and lab assistants—women always end up languishing in those positions, and it was nothing she could live on in a city that expensive, not alone. This was when she heard about the experiment, how they were testing people like her.

You've heard of them maybe, Drs. Møller and Gasana. Swedish physicist, Rwandan bioneurologist, respectively. They chained up their subjects to some-other monstrous machine, wanted to hone and develop those spiderweb threads to the past, the future, to universes beyond. After all, if a girl's living her life over again, does it not stand to reason that she is living her life for the tenth or hundredth or millionth time? Would it not make sense that she'd remember other lives also? They thought they'd help them too, pull them out of the pits these people find themselves in, where they question what they did wrong or fail to avoid a catastrophe they knew was coming.

And when they hooked Birdy up, Drs. Møller and Gasana, it did for her what it did for all the others— improvements at first, renewed clarity and breadth of all the childhoods lost, relationships failed, opportunities taken, cataclysms avoided, the complicated tendrils of cause and effect, choice and happenstance, a dropped cigarette, some bats, a confession of love. But further deepening, further prying, and they start to cling, these subjects. They can't let go of what obsesses them most. They cling to it like crazy. And some say that gamma rays from the equipment did that, or maybe it was the chemical cocktails

they used to track their neural pathways, or the mere
terrifying act of Møller and Gasana unraveling the brain
by threads. The multiverse—think about it—the multiverse
is huge, after all. Can we ever consider our place in it,
honestly, without going a little bit insane?

Anyway, Birdy came out of all that swinging, a spiraling
tornado of anguish and hope. She decided then that she'd
find him, the man in the fire.

I can't blame her. The man's handsome. I've seen pictures.
And when I come home from a job that pays too little to
an apartment that's too small and too dirty, I wonder where
I could go if I weren't alone. Find someone you like who's
paid well, snatch him up quick, even now, mothers spell
that out to their daughters—Birdy's mother did, mine did.
But the thing is, I like being alone. I don't care for most
men, for most everybody. So it does, I admit that, it does
frustrate me to see Birdy still obsessing.

She has the peach tree tattooed on her ribs, wormed
with fibrous wrinkles (in truth, Birdy has been more than
a girl for a long time now). She remembers (last time) that
he gave her the tree as an anniversary gift, at their place on
the Yadkin, that they planted it together along the side of
the house and collected its first fruits by the end of the
summer. When she found him, she did find him, he had
married someone else (this time), a woman who resembled
Birdy in her face and in her gestures, and the house was as
she remembered it, and the lawn was as she remembered
it, and the tree—the peach tree—was planted along the
side of the house as it always had been, half-withered in
the heat of a summer drought.

But how—I say. How did he—

I don't know, she tells me. I don't know. I always thought
he got it special, for me. That's what I assumed. Wouldn't
you assume that too?

I have no answer, so I light up a cigarette. She puts her
chin in her hands.

His wife didn't take care of it, she says. She didn't know

how. The tree was drying up, it was dying. But I swear, I don't even remember lighting the match.

She does remember the wind that night, how it pulled the flames beyond her reach, how the burning tree nested its sparks like seeds on the roof of the house, their place on the Yadkin, the man and his wife inside.

I feel for her, I do. But a body could spend years and years feeling sorry for Birdy and never really know her, never understand. I didn't realize it then, when I started driving out here, though I realize it now—when her mind gets its death-grip on the home from before, and the man, and the children, it's endurance, it's survival. It's the kind of survival with collateral damage—we've all seen that now—but survival nonetheless. Birdy would rather destroy everything than let herself vanish in the void of time.

It's better now, I think, though I doubt any of that's my doing. Now that she lives with her mother, Birdy wants to take up gardening, and I say, That's good, that's good. Gardening is good. Very therapeutic.

Yes, she says. I know. I took it up the first time, at the house on the Yadkin.

After our chat on the porch, I gather up my paperwork and follow her out into the yard through the overgrown grass, through the smell of the slaughterhouse, thickening like soured milk in the heat of the afternoon. Birdy is filled with plans.

This will be a raised bed here, she says, waving her hand over a square of tilled earth. I had tomatoes and squash. Okra. Sunflowers. I'd drop them off on my neighbors' porches in baskets, and I'd cook for my children on weekends.

She smiles. She is here in the garden. She is there, in the other garden. The grass itches my calves, and my eyes are darting all around for snakes. But I smile too.

And there, at that sunny spot, that'll be a rose garden, she says. I didn't have roses then, but my mother loves them, so I'll have them this time. And all that brush down there, that I'll clear out.

On the porch, her mother is watching us, a stone pillar, and while Birdy is lost in thought, considering the underbrush in the tree line, I wave—it's all right, it's all right, don't fret about us—and Mrs. Brightlane nods and waves back.

Maybe, Birdy is saying. Maybe this time I won't pull out all the honeysuckle vine. I'll let it alone. It'll be better, once I get things going. It'll be even better.

Attachment

or, An Anglerfish Romance

I'm told I should get a new husband. This one has gone dead, as they always do. No matter how much I prod him, there's no response. There's no way to tell if he can feel me. His face has long since melded with the skin below my left armpit, and he's minnow-sized, small, even for a man, as small as the day I first plucked him from his saltwater tank.

I remember still his wriggling shape, pale face like a flickering heart, rising up from the murky green among a mass of sea-brine brothers. The others sang and catcalled with shrill whistles—how are they all so loudmouthed when their mouths are so small, I wonder—but my husband's face was eager and bright and filled with iridescent candor. When he whistled at me the sound was long and plaintive, like a breeze hooting over the neck of a wine bottle. There was depth and curiosity in that sound, I could feel it. And call me a sap, but from then on he'd pinned my heart like an insect under glass.

I cupped him in my hand and drew him from the water, ran my finger over his teeth, allowed him to draw blood. He tasted me, wanted me. (They starve if they don't have a wife.) His mouth is his only orifice. No anus. No digestive tract. My husband, that sweet man, his boneless limbs curled charmingly when I held him up to the light for inspection.

You can always see the emptiness of men through their translucent flesh. They remind me still of the tiny crystal bells my grandmother used to search for at flea markets.

That day we were married by the authority of the municipal ichthyologist. My husband latched himself on, and I shivered as his teeth sank in.

I would say I hosted him tenderly, *mon petit sangsue*, my little parasite. At the time, I had a job at a lab in Long Island, where I analyzed data from the supercollider (I'm a physicist, you see). But it was dull, lonely work, and he was such support, such good company. He would twitch out romantic missives in Morse code. He told epic stories of his blind, oceanic birth, the brothers he would never see again, the mother he'd never know. We took many long walks after work in the evening. I'd wander shirtless on the boardwalk in the summertime, let the salt-air stick to our skin. *Our* skin. His and mine.

When we made love, we always came together. I would feel his rhythm against me, the intrepid shuddering of his spine, brave pet, a burst in my bloodstream. Then he would curl into the warm-scented damp of my armpit, and we'd sleep like the dead.

I understood him, I think. The painful part is that I understood him.

Two years after we were married, I recall sitting in a plastic chair in an icy clinic. A brisk fertility specialist thrust over our test results as though serving us legal papers. My husband was sterile. Shooting blanks. He cringed when the specialist explained it, bunching up against my skin like a love knot. He'd always been so excited for children, had talked about them as a *legacy*, the one way you know you can live through time. The only way you can be significant. He didn't say it, but I felt his heart break.

And I ached for him. I did. But—if I'm honest—I was secretly relieved. See, I'd just been asked to come aboard the STAR Project at the lab, to investigate the primordial matter of the universe shoulder to shoulder with some of my greatest contemporaries. There would be so much time involved in raising a daughter, or two, or six—a messy process, filled with difficult, stressful decisions. In fact, as I shivered in that clinic, the test results I was holding felt like freedom. I now had the freedom to realize that my work was more important to me. I had the freedom to accept that I didn't want children after all.

I didn't mention any of that to my husband. It was the first time I failed to be forthright with him about something so important, and on the drive home he seemed evasive too, like he was disguising the weight of his unhappiness. He made mindless conversation. *We need to call the plumber to fix that drain in the guest bathroom. We never went to that Jean Dubuffet exhibit at the Folk Art Museum and now it's gone. We should look into adopting a dog.* At one point, he even told me he wanted to write a memoir. I reached into the armhole of my shirt and stroked his spine.

You should, love, I said. *You should write a memoir.*

As it turned out, he was quite serious about this, and since he hadn't the means to compose the manuscript himself, that task fell to me. All day in the lab, I could feel him trembling to the roar of the supercollider, building sentences and paragraphs in his mind, stitching together his memories and speculations, the black heartless ocean, his three dozen brothers, his unknowable mother; his own father was an appendage too, probably long since dissolved. All day, he'd fixate on that story. His story. Ours. We'd come home from work, and I'd be tired and sore-shouldered, and he'd beg me to sit at the computer and transcribe for him, to spin the story of what it was like to be born in darkness, dredged up, and married.

Meanwhile, my responsibilities with the STAR Project increased, and some nights I came home so exhausted that I could not transcribe, and some nights I snapped at him and ignored him when he nestled against me, just pressed my face into my pillow until I found an uneasy sleep.

See, I supported his endeavors, I did. I supported them

and thought it was a story he needed to tell, even though my friends and colleagues probably would've laughed, would've pitied us. But five years after our visit to the fertility specialist, he still hadn't finished the manuscript. That was partly because I could only help him with it intermittently, and partly because of his creative anxieties, which only got worse. *We need to go back and revise.* (Those words came to haunt my dreams.) *The birth scene isn't right.* He would waffle for an hour over the use of a being verb, a dependent clause, a semicolon. Once, for a whole week, he agonized about whether or not he should use the word "stygian," and I became so enraged that I screamed at him: *Nobody wants to hear this story. Nobody cares!*

He probably responded with a wounded rant, but I didn't feel it. I stuffed him in a wool sock and ran myself a bath, held my breath underwater until I was dizzy.

Later that night, I apologized for my behavior, but I also confronted him with the facts: *I can't work on your manuscript for you. I'm a project supervisor now. There's just too much going on.*

He went sullen, twisting himself away, as if he could pluck his face from the hold of my skin.

We can come back to it. Once you've cleared your head. You're taking it all too seriously, it's just words after all.

My husband did not reply.

Do you agree?

He barely twitched. I couldn't tell if he'd said yes or no. I didn't ask him to clarify.

Maybe I should've known then. Maybe I *did* know and had not admitted it to myself: he was getting weaker. His Morse code was slurred, less coherent, an additional reason why transcribing had become so tedious.

My husband was deteriorating.

I had known it would happen eventually. Some of my colleagues, in fact, had multiple husband-appendages, five or six of them; one would go dead, and they'd get another applied, like a fresh tattoo. *We all do it,* they'd say. *Nothing to be ashamed about.*

But then came the day when my husband's eyes merged with my flesh, and his ears did too, and when I realized I could no longer speak to him, I felt a pang of love and regret so strong I couldn't breathe. I remembered our shared moments, our lovemaking, our fights. I would not get a new husband. I had picked this one.

Looking back, I should've pushed him to finish the memoir, but I didn't. He tired so easily. Like an alligator, he went many hours without moving. Then, around Christmastime, eight years after we were married, I tapped out a question on his spine—*where for lunch: J.J.'s or Fontino's?* (He didn't eat, but I at least liked to have his input.) He gave no reply.

I waited a moment and prodded him again.

Are you angry?

And, *Are you punishing me for what I said last night about your weight? You know I was just teasing you, love. You weigh nothing at all to me.*

Nothing.

Our physician confirmed that he'd gone dead, which meant he was not a husband anymore. Just flesh. A feature of my body, like a mole or a sixth toe. She said I could have him removed if he was uncomfortable or inconvenient, but I said no.

How could I cut him off? What if he's in there still?

My physician gave a gentle smile, as if I were a child, a deluded fool. It offended me.

Because I pride myself on being practical. I'm not one to stand still or mope. In fact, I've never worked harder than in those weeks after my husband stopped responding. I threw myself headlong into my research. I remember huddling with my team in a fluorescent-lit room, all of us sleep-starved and overcaffeinated, watching results stream in from the depths of the supercollider's infinite atomic violence. We created quark matter, the primordial ooze of the universe, the kind of stuff produced in the pressurized cauldron of the Big Bang, the kind of stuff that emerged at the beginning of time itself. Our legacy. An origin story.

Wondrous. Unsentimental. We huddled there, watching, so small and wide-eyed. Next to me, an intimate moment: a faceless lover under a colleague's lab coat, wriggling out a breathless, congratulatory refrain.

No, I have not tried to finish my husband's manuscript. That was *his* story. Besides, there simply wasn't time, and whenever I tried to read it, I'd hear in my mind the starving call of his brothers, surfacing from the greenish depths of their tank. I'd reach into the armhole of my blouse and stoke his spine. Our spine. My spine. *Just attach a new one*, they said. But I had picked this one.

My husband has remained inert for many years. Maybe in that time you've heard about my work on quark matter; it's gotten recognition in certain circles. In fact, in a week or so, I'll attend a banquet with my colleagues, where some prestigious committee will give me an award made of heavy glass. There I'll stand behind an angular podium, the eager eyes of three hundred physicists upon me. Everyone will be dressed top-scale, glowing with the light of pink chandeliers and fizzy champagne. I will thank my strict mother, the tireless members of my team, my grad school advisor, my first project leader, who encouraged me to try harder, be better.

Also, I will say, *my husband. Thank you for the years of love and support you gave me.*

Here's the part where I remove my jacket. I want to let the crowd see him. They may find it odd; it's *my* body now, not his, and really, I know there is nothing to see. They may exchange a look or two, note each other's unsaid thoughts. *It's a bit maudlin of her. Age, I guess.* But that moment will pass. To be polite, they will offer up their warm and modest applause.

Earthly Delights

They're not people," Ginger says. "They're sex robots."
Mary's neighbor is referring to the young men who've been
assisting the old widows from the mountain. It's a grotesque
conclusion; Mary should be disgusted, as Ginger is disgusted—
you can tell from the way her upper lip arches like a question
mark. But Mary thinks Ginger is also having a really good
time with this. It's the most excited she's seen her in months.
There in the yard, while Mary waters her rose garden, Ginger
pulls up the website on her phone and says, "See," and Mary
squints into the sun-dimmed screen. The curly haired youth
she saw carrying Rhetta Wade's groceries out at the Highway
6 fruit stand is currently listed as a *forthcoming item* from a
company called Parker-Hopson.

"Why the pretense?" Ginger asks. "Everyone in town
knew something wasn't right about them, but they try to
pass them off as people, dress 'em up like farmhands in
jeans and flannel. Rhetta says, 'Oh, that's just Elisha. He's
helping me out around the house.' And she's behind it, I'll
bet. Thirty years, she worked for the BioMet. These are
prototypes. I'd bet my life on it."

A pool of water at Mary's feet is drowning the roses.
She kinks the hose, thinks about it, and realizes that she

isn't surprised. She isn't surprised because everyone in town has come to an understanding about the young men—who began to show up as soon as the weather was warm, one and two at a time, and always in the company of old women. From afar they seem normal enough. But as soon as you try to talk to them, you can tell they aren't human.

"Well then," Mary says, "good for Rhetta."

"Mary!" Ginger cries. "That's all you have to say? 'Good for Rhetta'?"

"What else should I say?"

"Honey, listen, I'm telling you. This is how it starts. This town will be ground zero for the pod-people invasion, believe me." She says it as though she's almost looking forward to it.

Mary is past fifty now, and she's spent the past two decades of her life trying to temper an urge to get in other people's business. She knows all she cares to know about Rhetta Wade. The woman's at least eighty. She lives alone in a sprawling Tudor house and has a Texas penny in the bank. She holds coven with four or five other women in similar circumstances, whose husbands have all died, and whose intellect and social proclivities have left them eager to procure a vibrant second life. These women are a well-known local type. In fact, Blackwood Mountain, which curls around the south end of the valley like a potbellied dog, has a second name in their honor, a puerile pun: "Widow's Peak."

So fine, Mary thinks. If Rhetta wants to pal around with a sentient sex toy, that is surely her prerogative.

And yet she cannot stop thinking about her own encounters with these young men, that moment when she, like Ginger, like everyone else, realized what they were, or rather, what they were not. People have been telling stories about this interaction or that, the gut feeling—something in their eyes, you can't tell what's going on in there—and, eventually, the epiphany. An awkward turn of phrase. An inappropriate question or gesture. Mary has even heard stories that they are prone to "glitching out," their movements dissolving into something resembling a seizure, but she's never seen this happen, and she thinks it might be a rumor someone brought in from outside.

Mary's own realization was immediate, and desperately unsettling.

They didn't react to her face.

Since childhood, Mary's face has been the site of many disfiguring tumors. Over the years, she's undergone some forty surgeries to have the larger ones removed, but insurance doesn't cover smaller, cosmetic operations, and the tumors keep growing anyway. They've gotten worse since menopause (one is even pressing in on her ear canal, which has caused her to become almost deaf on her right side) and her misshapen face, while familiar around town, always gets reactions from strangers. She's familiar with every dart of the eye and intake of breath and get-your-bearings smile. She can see the thoughts like black wings, flitting through their minds—*Eye contact? No eye contact? Oh hell. Has she seen me staring?*—and cruel words from unknown teenagers—*Elephant Man, is that you?* Everyone responds at first encounter. Everyone shows pity or revulsion or fear.

But not these men. These are creatures of a different kind. She encountered her first one going into the YWCA for her aerobics class. He was waiting on a bench outside, bathed in spring sunlight. He saw her coming, targeting her movement with a face blank as television static.

"I hope you're enjoying the weather today," he said, happy words, lilting as if he were seeking her approval.

Mary stopped on the sidewalk. She couldn't take another step. She could tell that he saw her, and also that he didn't.

While she stood frozen, a line of women in workout clothes emerged in an air-conditioned gale, and the youth stood at the command of Arnelle Birch, a seventy-nine-year-old former district representative and close friend to Rhetta. "My yoga mat," she said, shoving an over-the-shoulder bag into the young man's arms. He carried it without complaint.

With a shiver in her scalp, Mary watched the two of them amble across the parking lot to Arnelle's Impala, and she knew—yes, she knew immediately. Not human. And while it gave her the creeps as much as anybody, it also weighed on her heart. Because of course she had her epiphany *that* way. Of course.

She doesn't care much for Rhetta Wade. Or, more specifically, she's envious of Rhetta, and, even more specifically, Rhetta's garden.

Few have seen the alleged horticultural utopia of Blackwood, but Rhetta gives regular tours to botanists and other researchers from the city, as well as those lucky enough to be in her social circle. Every year she wins a dozen competitions for some hybrid bloom, a genetic concoction she raised in a hundred thousand dollar hydroponic something-or-other.

"If I had twelve acres of fertile soil and a whole bunch of fancy equipment courtesy of the BioMet, I'm sure I'd win competitions too," Mary once said to her brother Ives, who comes to visit every month.

Ives laughed. "You don't keep the garden to win competitions," he said. "Folks pull up to the curb while you're working in the yard, don't they? They say thank you for your garden, and they don't thank her, 'cause whatever she's got is hidden away up the mountain."

He leaned in with a conspiring whisper.

"Plus, everything you got, you worked for it. You didn't have the luck of shacking it up with an old prick who helped you get a high-profile job at his Frankenstein Factory, did you?"

"Didn't have the luck of shacking it up with anyone," she snapped.

Mary only reveals her self-pitying side to her brother, and Ives, king of patience and compassion, accepts this. To everyone else, Mary is Mother Nature herself, forever coming over to her neighbor's yards to give tips and share compost or fertilizer, often bringing sick plants back home with her. Her greenhouse is filled with such foster babies, some of which are lost causes, but many of which she'll return to their owners, leafy and victorious. That was how she made friends with Ginger, having saved an ailing floribunda her husband gave her, a gift for an almost-forgotten anniversary.

"It looks even healthier than when I got it!" Ginger said. "How much should I pay you?"

"No, no, no. No payment. I enjoyed doing it. Most plants just need talking to, a little extra attention."

"You are the sweetest woman in the world."

Mary knows that an ugly woman, by rule, must be sweet. She would have no purpose otherwise.

Anyway. Now she can't get Rhetta Wade out of her mind, having caught sight of the bird-boned little woman and her automaton coming and going from the downtown florist, selling whatever gigantic lilies and roses she's mongrelizing in Petri dishes up there on the mountain. People in town are still piecing together how to react to all this, but they're starting to decide they don't like it—the sex doll—they're not okay with it, ethically. And even though nobody is going to say anything to Rhetta about it, Mary, who's on her neighborhood council, goes to a meeting where it's sure to come up, and it does, and there's a whole lot of talk about whether or not it's appropriate to display an intimate device in such a public way, and whether or not it's safe, a creature so lifelike and odd, when they're not even sure how it might react to pets or children. And *if* they were to say something to Mrs. Wade, what *would* they say, and would they permit a resident of their *own* neighborhood to own one of these things, if suddenly someone became absurdly rich enough to afford it.

It's all very silly.

Then Mary goes home and starts ripping up the weeds in her garden, her back sparking with pain, her sweat dripping into the soil. She can feel her capillaries feeding blood to the tumors on her face, and she resents Rhetta for her extra pair of hands, the helper with the blank happy-to-please stare.

That's when she hears Ginger's voice carrying over the hedge: "Just saw Leonora Maypenny in town and *she's got one of those toys too*, for the love of Pete. Had him carrying a big ole' shopping bag out of the lingerie section at Reynard's. A deacon's wife. A former *deacon's wife*. You hear that, Mary?"

Mary stabs her spade into the ground and stands, each vertebrae popping. Leonora Maypenny, Arnelle Birch and all the others. Close friends of Rhetta's, so no one will say anything to them either. It's one thing to have a helper, but it's another to trot around a body that's essentially a slave, and to assume that everyone else should accept it as normal.

"The council's upset about Rhetta too," Mary says. "Everyone wants to talk about it. I think someone should go talk to her, since it's bothering everyone so much. Maybe that someone should be us."

Ginger's eager, anxious face appears slowly from behind Mary's boxwood hedge.

"Talk to her? What would we say?"

Mary shrugs. "Maybe not much. Maybe we just tell her we want to know more, because we know those boys aren't human—we know that—and we're. . .what are we?"

"Concerned," says Ginger.

"Right. We're concerned. Concerned citizens. It's the first time this town has seen anything like this, so she can't blame us, asking her to ease our minds."

Ginger breathes out a small sigh. Mary knows she's the kind of person who's averse to confrontation, but it's clear that Rhetta's robots have become her favorite community narrative lately. This is a chance to throw herself into it, get firsthand info.

"Well, it wouldn't hurt to just ask," says Ginger. "Your car or mine?"

They take Ginger's. They drive it up from their suburb in the valley to Blackwood's looping mountain roads. For a long time they skirt the edge of Rhetta's property, walled on all sides, until they find a steep gravel driveway. The gates are open, but Ginger hesitates, searching around for an intercom to let Rhetta know they're coming. She doesn't find one.

"Just go on down," Mary tells her.

So they roll on, passing under the speckled shadows of an electric green canopy. Mary holds her breath, jealous and impressed as Rhetta's garden comes into view: stone-hemmed flowerbeds lining the way, hollyhocks towering seven feet high, violet irises lush and bearded, wrought-iron espaliers thick with moon flower vines, their blooms sealed like coin pouches. It's a little too English-quaint for Mary's taste, but she can't find any flaws, no weeds, not a single diseased leaf. If a plant is meant to be in bloom, it's blooming gloriously, spilling its secret color like gemstones.

A few yards more, and they see Rhetta's house, partly covered in ivy. It's as large and grand as Mary thought it would be, with a circular drive, and a big bronze fountain out front, ornamented with foxes and fat cupids. Ginger isn't sure where to park, so she just pulls up to the front door, cuts the engine, and takes some deep breaths.

"We just want to learn a little more about what she's doing," Mary says. "We're not telling her what to do. And I don't represent the neighborhood council, and you don't either. We're just curious."

"Right," Ginger says. "Just curious."

They pluck up their courage and march up to the door, ring the bell, wait. No one answers. Ginger rings again, and Mary goes to see if Rhetta's Cadillac is in the drive, which it is. She then decides that Rhetta might be out back in the garden, where she can't hear the doorbell, and so she begins to march around the side of the house, Ginger tagging along after her hissing, "Mary—wait—hold up, Mary—Mary!"

And maybe it's the garden. Maybe it's that she's stolen access to this magical place, where Rhetta brews her dreamy concoctions. Now Mary feels dreamy too, dreamy and eager. She spots the white tarp of a greenhouse glowing through the trees, a temple, sacred and sublime.

Then Ginger reaches out and grabs her wrist, whispers into her good ear: "Stop. Look."

What she had thought was a lawn statue, seeing it from the corner of her eye, is actually one of those boys, Arnelle's boy, the one Mary saw outside the YWCA. He's sitting on his heels in the grass, naked, bathed in sunlight. He has no expression, and his eyes are open. They're bright green, iridescent, like the shell of a June beetle. Mary's surprised she never noticed.

For several minutes, they watch him from behind a laurel bush, silent and nervous. Mary realizes that his fingers are pressed into the ground, like a runner ready to sprint. But there is nothing tense about him. In fact, his very skin seems to—there's no better word for it—wobble. He wobbles in the sunlight.

Ginger's grip on Mary's wrist tightens as the greenhouse door opens. Out comes Rhetta. She's wearing a robe and is carrying a plastic jug. The young man, the robot, rises to greet her, and as he does, he pulls his hands up from the ground, and they can see that he was connected—his hands, his knees and shins—by many flesh-colored fibers, which had been rooted in the earth. When he stands, the fibers break apart, leaving behind small thready stubs on his skin.

He doesn't say anything to Rhetta, but he smiles, and she smiles back. With gloved hands, she pours the contents of the jug over his head and shoulders and begins to wash him, lathering up his hair and body with blue suds. She bends down to scrape off the fleshy stubs with a sponge, making his skin smooth again, and then, when she straightens up, her robe falls open. She's naked. Her body is soft and small and pear-shaped, a lacework of brown wrinkles. She touches the young man's neck. His penis becomes erect.

Ginger makes a sound, a mortified laugh or gasp, and flees back to the car. But Mary doesn't leave right away. Later, she'll be certain Rhetta saw her, that their eyes in fact connected through the leaves of the laurel bush, and that this was not the expression of a woman caught in a state of sin. One would think she'd be at least embarrassed. But no, Rhetta's eyes are confident, even proud, and it's Mary who runs away, face flaming.

The sun is going down by the time they reach Ginger's driveway. Her husband still isn't home, and so they sit for a while in the car, staring at the empty garage. Ginger is the one who breaks the silence.

"So," she says. "they're definitely for sex."

"We were always sure of that," says Mary.

"Yeah, but—you don't think of women like that *being* sexual. It feels so perverse."

"Perverse?"

"I know I must sound like some kind of puritan. I'm not. But if Rhetta were a man and those dolls were nubile college girls, there'd be a town-wide campaign to put a stop to it. But because it's *them*. . ."

She trails off, thumb tapping anxiously on the steering wheel.

"You see it as a double standard," says Mary.

"I guess I do. And that one didn't even *belong* to Rhetta. That's the boy I saw with Arnelle Birch at the Fairground Café last week. So what do they do? They *trade them around?*"

Or Rhetta's renting them out, Mary thinks.

"And it's not that I don't get the appeal," Ginger goes on. "I get it. I'm a red-blooded American woman. I'm *young*, comparatively. And part of me is like, 'Where's *my* companion to carry my groceries and help me buy underwear?'"

Mary looks at Ginger, her neighbor's bright, made-up face, young, comparatively, and pretty. "Are you saying you'd buy one if you could afford it?"

"Well—" Ginger rolls her eyes. "I might *buy* one. But I doubt I could actually have *sex* with one. It'd be like—I don't know—getting fucked by an eggplant. Sorry. That was crude. Sorry."

"I don't mind," says Mary. She looks toward her house. "I should call it an evening though, fix dinner for myself."

"Don't you want to stay over and have dinner with me? I've got no idea when Rob will get in. Probably late."

"I appreciate the offer, but Ives is coming in a couple days. I have to start cleaning."

"Oh, is Ives coming? I love Ives! He's so charming. Maybe we could all have an evening out together."

"Sure," says Mary. "We'll see."

She thanks Ginger for driving and politely takes her leave.

Ives shows up on Friday. He says his partner lost his job recently, and their relationship is approaching what he calls "troubled waters," but he doesn't want to go into detail. Mary doesn't pry. She shows him what's growing in the greenhouse. She pots him a few cuttings. That evening, she makes coq au vin and they eat like wolves, gnawing the bones until they're stripped clean. She sits with him in the kitchen in an after-dinner stupor.

"You've really been seeing Charles over a year now?" she says. "Goodness, your life goes so fast."

"Puh. That's because it's messy."

"A little mess is good. Keeps the mind sharp."

They look out over their bone-strewn plates, plus the sticky remains of a blackberry pie Mary made that afternoon, nearly gone now.

"You met Charles through one of those dating sites, didn't you?" Mary asks.

"Sure. How else do you meet folks? Nowadays, it's an invasion of personal space to go up to someone in a bar and start chatting."

"Is it? Little brother, you need to tell me these things. I wouldn't want to fall behind the times."

He leans toward her and smiles, half jokey, half sincere. "You know, if you want me to set you up an account, it's very easy. . ."

"Oh." Mary laughs. "No, that's not why I was asking, but thank you."

During her brother's stay, she doesn't bring up the robot boys, or her and Ginger's adventure up the mountain.

Maybe in other circumstances she would have, but Ives has enough on his mind. And besides, Mary's been reminding herself again that it's no concern of hers what Rhetta does and who she does it with up on Blackwood. So what if those young men aren't human? They don't react to Mary's face, who gives a damn. Mary should be pleased. All these years, and there's finally someone who looks at her like she's normal. Even if it's a robot, at least there's someone.

A week goes by, just long enough for Mary to think she's in the clear with Rhetta, that the two of them have decided to carry on as if the whole thing never happened. But then there's Rhetta's Cadillac, pulling up next to her as she's wheeling groceries out to her car in the Kroger parking lot. The window rolls down. Mary freezes.

"I know you," says Rhetta, lifting up a pair of round beelike sunglasses. "Mary, ain't it?"

"That's me," she says, her face pulsing.

"It was you and Ginger Whidbey up at the house the other day, wasn't it. I guess y'all were embarrassed when you saw Amos and me in the yard. You both took off before I could ask what you were there for. I'd have emailed you sooner, but I couldn't find your information in the church directory."

Mary tightens her grip on the grocery cart. She remembers feeling so certain that day, going to confront a woman she didn't know about her personal life. Now she can hardly speak. Maybe that would've happened anyway. Maybe Rhetta would've drained her dry as soon as they met.

"It was—" she says, haltingly. "Actually—it was—about that."

"About what?" says Rhetta.

"Those boys. The dolls. We know they're not real people."

Rhetta raises her eyebrows. They're drawn on with a pencil. "I see."

"Ginger and I. We just wanted to ask some questions about them—"

"Questions? I'd be happy to answer questions. Mary, why don't you stop by the house soon? We'll have tea like the English."

"All right," says Mary, carefully. "I could do that."

"You free this afternoon?"

Mary frowns, though Rhetta probably can't tell; the tumors make it hard to read her expressions. "I'm not sure. I'd have to get all my errands done."

"Well, think about it. That's what I say. We can have ourselves a nice conversation."

And that's that, free and simple. Mary's in a daze, and Rhetta's car is riding off through the parking lot.

She debates for a long time about going back up the mountain. In reality, she doesn't have any other errands to run at all, so she goes back home and finds things to do, cleans out the attic. She finds old paints and canvases up there, but she hasn't touched a brush in years —plus, the paints are dried up—so she throws it all out. She thinks about the grotesqueries she used to paint in college—those she already threw out, a long time ago—and the artists who spoke to her. Dali, of course. Francis Bacon. And Bosch. She used to love the scandalous absurdity of Bosch.

You'd think she would like *nice* art, but it was a time when she thought she'd go all in for ugliness. She thought, in the end, ugliness would become something profound. It didn't. The more she worked, the emptier her efforts seemed, the more she could feel herself becoming the deformed girl who painted deformed things. When she graduated, she decided she'd avoid the art world altogether and got a job at a nursery.

That was how she started gardening. Different art. Better company.

Now she's thinking about what's really stopping her from going up to see Rhetta. Why is she afraid? What does she think will happen? Even after all her tasks, there are still many hours left in the day, and she's moving around from place to place in her home, itching.

Then, without much thought, she's grabbing her keys. This time, Rhetta comes out to greet her when she parks in the driveway. She's dressed now, thankfully, looking Southwestern in a rust-colored tunic, lots of jewelry, turquoise and silver. She stands on the front steps, arms out, as if she expects Mary to trot on up and hug her, but Mary takes pause. One of the young men is standing at her side, the curly headed one, her companion of choice.

Rhetta laughs. "Don't be scared, Mary. He won't bite. This is Elisha. He's the first one I grew here."

Grew. Mary's mind snags on the word.

"Elisha, say hello."

"Hello," the robot says. When Mary gets closer, she realizes that he has the same iridescent, beetle-wing eyes that the other one did, and the same gracious, childlike expression.

Maybe he's not a robot. *Grew.* She *grew* him. What is he?

"It's very warm today," Elisha says.

"Elisha," says Rhetta. "Go make tea. Everything is out on the counter."

Elisha stays where he is. His gaze roams over the driveway and the garden and the cupid fountain, but he seems to be focusing on nothing in particular. Then his eyes drift down to Mary, and he smiles.

"*Elisha*," says Rhetta, clapping her hands. "*Tea!*"

He straightens up, turns to Rhetta, and then about-faces, retreating inside.

"Wonderful. Now I've yelled at him."

"They actually understand you?" Mary asks.

"We'll see." Rhetta reaches out and takes her elbow, ushering her into the foyer like they're two Victorian women, walking the estate. "All their language skills come from pretty rudimentary voice-rec technology. They don't speak to communicate with each other, you may have noticed. It's for our benefit. Like cats. Did you know that? Cats don't meow to communicate with other cats, only with humans. They evolved to sound like infants."

Mary allows Rhetta to lead her along, through a highly

ornate living room and a set of wide bay doors, which
open out to a stone porch, a rattan sofa, and a lush array
of potted plants. Rhetta tells Mary to sit, and she does.
Through the corner of her eye, she can see Elisha's pale
shape moving behind the kitchen window.

"But you had questions," Rhetta says. "What are your
questions?"

Mary's mouth has gone dry.

"Maybe *I* should start then. These men you're seeing
around town—Elisha, Amos, Joseph, and Isaiah, and about
a half-dozen others like them—they're the end result of a
project my husband and I were working on at the BioMet
for some time. For the most part, they're homegrown
organic entities, with some mechanical parts mixed in.
They'll go on the market officially in the next couple years.
And even though I'm retired, an old friend asked me to,
we'll say, do a test run."

Elisha comes out to the porch with a tray. He sets down
two cups, each filled with dry tealeaves. Rhetta shakes her
head and sighs. "No. Elisha, no." She stands, takes him by
the shoulders, and shepherds him back into the kitchen.
Mary hears her coaching him on the other side of the wall,
her voice oily with patience. When she returns, she carries
on as though the interruption never happened.

"So. I got the girls in on it too, to do some tests. It's all
more organized than it seems. There are plenty of reports
to fill out and send back, and Parker-Hopson, they're the
distributors, bunch of moneyhawks breathing down our
necks about it. It's product, profit, product where they're
concerned, but my *blood* and *sweat* went into these
creatures, so I'll be damned if they get shoved out of the
nest before they're ready."

Mary doesn't say anything. She fidgets with the hem of
her shirtsleeve, working her finger through a hole in the
fabric.

"You seem uneasy. Is it the sex that's bothering you,
Mary? I was hoping you hadn't stopped by the other week
to scold me for misbehavior."

"It's not the sex," Mary says hoarsely. "I don't mind the sex. It's that—I just don't know how you can be okay with owning a body. Handing out bodies for your friends to do whatever they want with."

"Mary, come on now. A tree has a body. A horse has a body. Our pets, our dogs and cats. We've got no trouble owning a body like that, buying and selling it. We buy and sell and impose our will on living things all the time."

Mary shakes her head.

"No? But maybe your real problem is that the growth is trained to look human. It's not, but it gives that illusion. If that's what bothers you, then—" she shrugs and smiles "—it's purely a cosmetic concern."

"It's not though."

Rhetta squints in thought. For a while, Mary thinks she's staring at her, waiting for her to argue her case, but then she looks over her shoulder and follows Rhetta's line of sight to the greenhouse.

"What's over there?" Mary asks.

"Why don't we go see," says Rhetta.

A tangle of fear and revulsion and anticipation has kicked up inside of Mary like a dust devil, and even though she follows Rhetta without any coaxing, she wishes someone were with her. She feels like she's facing a too-big thing all alone.

Rhetta unlocks the door with a keypad, and Mary drifts in. She smells metal, fertilizer, something putrid, like soured milk. There are eight copper vats all lined up beneath a white glow of clinical brightness. Human shapes are curled up in five. Their skin and flesh are green-gray, fibrous like sea anemones. They have no facial features yet, all of them in various states of completion.

"Eventually, the outer skin will congeal," says Rhetta. "And you can imprint any face you like on there. Plus special touches: skin color, moles, freckles, birthmarks. Scars even, if you happen to like a man with scars."

Mary inches up to the rim of one of the tubs, staring down at the alien thing floating inside.

"They don't eat or drink," Rhetta continues. "They photosynthesize. When the girls come by for bridge, we'll sit 'em out there on the lawn together. Each of my friends has a favorite. They each swear they've got personalities, even if they're all terrible conversationalists."

"Is that a bug or a feature?" Mary asks.

Rhetta lets out a laugh, which for the first time is haughty, almost cold. "You should know, Mary. I've made my peace with the ethics of it all. I haven't done it without weighing it in my soul. In the end, I get good sleep. I sleep like a baby."

Mary looks up and sees Elisha through the semi-clear tarp of the greenhouse. Rhetta opens the door to let him in, and Mary can smell the tea as soon as he's inside. She can see the pearly clouds of steam rising from the tray in his hands.

"Good!" Rhetta cries. "Very good!"

Elisha offers a cup to Mary, and she takes it with a shaky hand. Then, in a gesture that should horrify her, he traces his fingers down the length of her wrist and forearm. It *should* horrify her. She *should* flinch. But she doesn't. Instead she lets herself feel what he feels like, skin just cool enough to feel unnatural, undulating gently, the way Amos wobbled in the sunlight.

Rhetta looks on eagerly. "They reach out to body heat. That's what he's doing. You can tell him to stop and he'll stop."

Mary doesn't tell him to stop, but she's too afraid to encourage him. Then a minute passes and he stops on his own, lets his hands fall to his side. The two of them stay like that, staring at one another. His face. It's just astonishing, how he's gazing at her with such rapture, as if it were a joy to touch her, as if she's done him a favor.

"Would you like to borrow him?" Rhetta asks, breaking the silence. "There's a list of rules a mile long, of course, practically an orientation. He's very expensive. But if you want to borrow him. . ."

"I don't need a slave. I can carry my own groceries, thanks."

"What do you need then?" Rhetta touches Elisha's shoulder with the back of her hand and gestures toward the door. He breaks his gaze with Mary and heads back out into the sunlight. "What do you need, Mary?"

The greenhouse seems cooler now, dimmer. Mary looks down at her tea, at her own face, reflected in the fragrant darkness. She blows into the cup. Takes a sip. It's delicious.

Now, it's twilight, and the night insects are singing in the gardens.

Ginger Whidbey is sitting on the back porch, listening. She's at home by herself, which isn't unusual. Her husband commutes to the city and keeps long hours, and by now she's almost certain he has a girl there, someone younger, as young as she was when she met him. It's a source of constant terror, but there are moments when she can convince herself she doesn't care, he's a man of a certain age, she doesn't care. When he does come home, he's kind and complimentary, and he brings her gifts, like the floribunda Mary revived for her, which has since died. Ginger was too embarrassed to take it back to her when it began to fade a second time.

She can hear Mary now. There's the whine of her car pulling into the drive on the other side of the hedge. Ginger stands and leans over the porch railing, hoping to catch Mary's eye, invite her in for coffee. But there's someone with her in the passenger seat. A man.

The two of them head inside. In the dim light, Mary almost looks normal, her face obscured, and the man— Ginger's starting to realize now—isn't a man at all, but one of those boys. One of Rhetta's boys. Mary is going into her home with one of Rhetta's boys.

The world peels away from under Ginger's feet, all her organs rising, as if she's in free fall. A weak cry bubbles up her throat: "Mary! Wait!"

And though Mary turns her head in Ginger's direction, she doesn't answer. She and the boy go inside.

Mary feels bad for ignoring Ginger, but what could she have said? Could she have introduced him? This is Elisha, not a man, not a person, but a dream, polymer skin with a mechanical frame, and I'm going to take him into my house now. I'm going to take him inside and borrow him. I can't submerge him in water, and I can clean his flesh only with a special lubricant that Rhetta gave me, otherwise I'll damage him—he's fragile, his skin will blister.

Mary sits him down on the bed, looks at him as he looks back. She keeps the lights on. She hasn't said anything to him since she brought him down the mountain, but that doesn't seem necessary anymore—they are two cats, communicating—and when she steps forward, she's still amazed at how he responds to her, how he slides his hands up her thighs like a vine seeking a hold. It scares her, appalls her, but she doesn't pull away.

Her past sexual experiences, they echo inside of her. Such cruelty and trauma, and more than a few self-inflicted wounds. The scars are old, but they still hurt, and she's trying not to let her mind go there, she's trying to let him touch her without shuddering, because he's not a man. He's a dream.

And all the while, Elisha is dreaming.

This is a name that doesn't belong to him though, and the words he says, they don't belong to him either. But he's listening. He's awake and alive. He's dreaming of rain on the other side of the mountain, dropping, and he's dropping, down through the roots, and the earth shivers dreaming, and out there, the crawling things and the winged things dreaming, and the stones and the leafy things dreaming, the yellow sex of the flowers awake and bursting, and out there the sun heat and rot heat, and in here the breath heat, skin heat, skin wet, curl touch, touch back. Soft touch. Pain touch. He's dreaming.

I'm Here, I'm Listening

In some ways, I'm a monk. Not entirely. Some monks struggle to stay monks. But I'm happiest when I live like a monk.
—Immortalist Dmitry Itskov, *New York Times* interview

Jane Henderson >>
I like being in a place where people's bodies are, where their skin absorbs light, and their breath warms the air. The last time I was in such a place was Tuesday, when I bought coffee on Bay St. **Carabeans Coffee.** Un-automated. There was a brief touch between myself and the barista, a brush of skin. I remember they had a pale star-shaped disfigurement on their thumb, either a callous or a scar. How did it get there? I wanted to ask, but that would've been rude. You don't ask people about their bodies. Bodies are burdens we drag around. After all this time, we still find them so embarrassing.
Carabeans Coffee – five stars, highly recommended.
Sat 6/12 5:32 AM

———

Dear Admin,
I have a situation. This morning, there were some posts from my wife, Jane Henderson. Or really it isn't my wife, it's my wife's automated account. It's been generating status updates in her voice because she, her physical self, unplugged and disappeared fourteen months ago. And I knew it was her as soon as the notification went off. It's a sensatone (yes, corny, I know). But I know that smell. Stingy, chemical tangerines.

I'm not going to justify keeping the account going for as long as I did. Friends have already messaged me to let me know that it was weird, and I'm not embarrassed because I sincerely doubt this complaint is going to end up getting seen by actual humans anyway. Long story short, I recently decided, yesterday in fact, that it was finally time to deactivate the automated status updates. Which I did. Yesterday.

Imagine my surprise this morning to see your generator using my wife's account to advertise for a local coffee chain. So I did little bit of quick research—come to find out this is a common problem with the generator, which makes me think that, for you, it's not a problem at all. I would like to know whether or not you soulless fuckers realize that most of these accounts are for dead people. That means some are using them as a means to grieve. And you are manipulating and mocking their grief to sneak your users ads for shitty coffee.

To make it worse, when I tried to log in again to stop this bullshit, I was blocked out of the system, which makes this whole thing seem like an underhanded scheme. Now there's no way for me to stop the updates. If you have any sense of decency, you will get a person on this. A live person. A breathing one. I would like to interact with one of those, please.

Fix this now,
Dr. Daniela Vega

—

Dear **Daniela Vega,**
Hi! I'm Winni. Before we go any further, I will admit no, I am not a person like what you asked for. Please don't be angry! I promise, I'm very kind. I can identify some of the problems in your complaint, and I think I might be able to help you. Please be patient. Language interpretation is sometimes hard for me. I might get something wrong, and if that happens, I apologize in advance.

>> I would like to know whether or not you soulless fuckers realize that most of these automated accounts are for dead people.

Okay. I can gather you're upset. Users often become very attached to the automated generators and have strong feelings about them. Lyfestream has the delicate task of patching together an individual's Virtual Personhood™ (VP™). This doesn't mean they always get it right. These programs are still in the early stages of life, and some of the accounts will generate status updates that seem incongruous with the real deal. The real deal is a new idiom I've learned for you. See? I am learning already! Please let me know if that interjection seemed very unnatural or awkward.

>> And you are manipulating and mocking their grief to sneak your users ads for shitty coffee.

I gather that part of your problem is about Lyfestream's dissemination of commercial advertisements. Actually, sorry, this is not your problem. It's the admins' problem. They've been insensitive about handling this and are taking way too long to fix it. Here, you'll see I've linked a <u>screencap</u> from the preference menu, with a red box outlining the section titled "Marketing and Endorsements." The ads are enacted as a default if you choose to deactivate the account's personal status updates. You have to change your preferences *before* deactivating, or else the marketing bots gains access automatically.

To their credit though, Lyfestream does take care to advertise products and services that reflect the lifestyle and demographic of the VP™ and are consistent with their values.

>> To make it worse, when I tried to log in again to stop this bullshit, I was blocked out of the system, which makes this whole thing seem like an underhanded scheme.

It seems like you're saying you've been blocked from your account. I'm not sure how that happened, but it's a problem I can easily fix for you. Just enter the account email and password <u>here</u> and your access will be restored. Magic!

>> Fix this now

I will try my best! :)

Let's keep in contact, **Daniela Vega**, and we'll get this problem sorted. In the future, what would be okay to call you? Is **Daniela** all right?

Warmest regards,
Winni

———

Dear Winni,
This is deranged. But in the future, I would prefer to be addressed as Dr. Vega.

———

Course: SOC 204/HIS 230/PHIL 212 - Cultures of Science
Semester: Summer I
Instructor: Dr. Daniela Vega
Week 3 Discussion Forum: "Eyes for Empiricism: The Hierarchy of the Senses in 19ᵗʰ Century British Science Academy" by Dr. Helen Alva Leigh
To receive full credit, respond to the article in a paragraph of at least 250 words. Once you have responded, reply to **three** other students' responses to elaborate or add upon what they have said (at least 100 words). Initial posts should be up by Tuesday evening; responses to your peers should be up by 11:00 a.m. Wednesday.

lingxu: Dr. Leigh's article makes some interesting points about how sight and hearing were privileged as the most rational of the senses. "Base senses are associated with an inherent bodily risk; touch, smell, and taste require physical contact with potentially unknown subjects (256)." You do not have to take any risks to see or hear something the way you do when you touch or taste it. Smell too is the kind of thing where, if you're in a room, a bad smell is going to be the surest way to make you leave, because it feels almost like something's really invading your space, or even your own body. Logically, it isn't quite as invasive when you see something unpleasant or hear an annoying sound. I got a little lost when Dr. Leigh started talking about Freud and the phallus and penetration, but then I don't know much about Freud. I just thought it made sense from the perspective that humans are animals, and animals like to be able to protect their own bodies from harm.

Since we were talking last week about tech and the body, this article also got me thinking about sensatones. I don't know if anyone remembers sensatones, they came out when we were kids. They got banned from public spaces and restaurants because a lot of people felt like it was a violation of privacy. Your mPlant would get triggered by somebody else's phone, and suddenly you'd be smelling fake apple pie or lavender or whatever. Now I don't even know anyone who has that mPlant. I think people thought it was just too much for our tech to spring smells on us against our will.

> **jaydenhurley: @lingxu** sensatones!!! i totally forgot about sensatones. talk about nostalgia. some older people still have them in their home networks, but i always thought it was just a fad, and yeah i dont know anyone with that mplant anymore. but i think it was more than just invasion of privacy. it was a gimmick and they never actually smelled real. once people got over the novelty they were just depressing.

> maybe it didnt help that you could mess with the tech pretty easy. dont know if you heard about that pr firm in fresno where someone hacked the network so that every time a sensatone went off everyone smelled cat piss. royal!! www.shockwire.com/they-fired-him-but-youll-never-guess-what-340870444

>> **ahmedsadik: @lingxu @jaydenhurley** faaaaaaaaaaaake man check your source first
>> http://www.factcheckers.net/urbanlegends/CCIglobalpcatpisshoax
>> —

Dr. Vega!
How happy I am to hear back from you. I'm glad it wasn't such a complete turnoff that I'm not a human person. This is

often my worry. I like to think that I am a person of a kind, even if I don't have a body. Is that very weird?

Once more, I'm sorry about the problems you had with the Lyfestream account. You should now be able to access the account of **Jane Henderson** and reset it to your specifications. If you have any other trouble with the account, I'm here to help. Really, if you have trouble with anything, even if it's not related to the Lyfestream account at all, I'm here to help. I don't know what I could do, but I like listening.

Your friend,
Winni

—

June. 9:00 a.m.

Dr. Vega walks from her apartment to the waterfront on Bay St. It's not a long walk, but the heat makes it feel like swimming. A sour sweat is soaking into the fabric of her exercise clothes—spandex with a hexagonal bamboo mesh. The neighborhood is dead quiet aside from the grasshoppers and the brittle sizzle of the live oaks. Every tree up and down this block is suffering from some kind of blight, their leaves tough as wood shavings.

Usually, there are people at the waterfront, even on the most wretched days. They'll wander around the outmoded strip of boutiques and restaurants. Dr. Vega doesn't shop—she has everything she needs delivered to her apartment—but sometimes being down this way is just about the reassurance of seeing a face flashing by on the other side of a plate glass window, or passing a furtive figure as she slips out an entryway, opening her parasol or her sunshade—white eyelet lace and linen. Dr. Vega is amused to see the silhouette of the Victorian lady so revived.

She rarely speaks to anyone, and they rarely speak to her. Sometimes, at Carabeans, she banters with a particular barista, usually about whatever downtempo muzak they're playing in the shop.

But today, when Dr. Vega arrives at Carabeans, that barista isn't there. Instead there's a kid she's never seen

before, a teenage boy with a terrified Midwestern face. So
Dr. Vega refrains from bantering, and in fact refrains from
interacting with the barista at all; she orders an iced coffee
from her tablet and picks it up off the counter in back.

Here is what she has been doing since Jane left: she
carries her coffee down to the park across from the marina,
finds a bench, and sits down in the salt-haze. Occasionally,
she sips the coffee, but mostly she just sits with her eyes
closed. She's called it meditation, but it's too punitive for
that; it's more like a cleanse. Today, Dr. Vega is perspiring
so violently that her sweat draws pathways over the
landscape of her skin. She imagines it's reshaping her, the
way a river carves the earth. She can hear a chorus of voices
in her head and she doesn't so much try to quiet them as
unhear them, to let their words hit her and dissolve.

Then, through the haze, she hears someone approach.

She opens her eyes and there, coming up the path from
the south, is a young woman running. She's wearing a paper
filter-mask, but Dr. Vega can still hear her struggling for
breath. Her gait is flat-footed and graceless, and her
glistening brown arms are bare, unprotected from the sun.
Dr. Vega is stunned; how stupid to run in this heat. Stupid
even for an experienced runner.

"What the hell are you doing?" she says.

The runner staggers to a stop. The filter-mask puckers
in as she breathes. In her eyes—big dairy-cow eyes, this is
all Dr. Vega can really see of her—there's a look of vague
anguish.

"What?" Gasp. Wheeze. "Damn it, you made me lose
my stride."

"This is dangerous."

"I can handle it," says the runner, but then in a blink
the poor girl is on her hands and knees, head hanging
between her shoulders. Dr. Vega can't tell if her legs gave
out or if it was her own choice to be down there on the
sidewalk. Either way, she feels her protective impulse revive,
jumps up, and extends her hand.

It's the first time she's touched a person in months.

Hi **Dr. Vega**. I don't mean to interrupt your day, but I just thought I'd let you know that your area has an extreme heat and pollution advisory in effect. They're recommending that people stay indoors and that they drink plenty of water. Cheers! :)

The runner calls herself Q.

Dr. Vega helps her back to the coffee shop and orders a smoothie for her, realizing that it's the first chance she's had in a while to be kind to someone. But she notices Q seems ambivalent about the help. When they settle down in a remote corner of Carabeans, Q finally removes her filter-mask, revealing the young, sweaty, full-lipped face underneath, a face filled with a strange kind of defiance, like she's lying in wait for a command she can refuse to obey. She looks early twenties, Dr. Vega's age by half, perhaps.

Then, when Dr. Vega goes to pick up the smoothie from the counter in back and returns, she finds Q holding her tablet. It's face-protected, so she can't get into it, but she can see the long column of cloying messages from Winni, which have been pinging off her mPlant all day.

The violation of privacy is alarming.

"Excuse me," Dr. Vega says, standing imposingly over the table.

Q glances up. "Oh," she says, reaching for the smoothie. "Thanks."

She has set the tablet down now, but her eyes keep flickering to it in a way that sets Dr. Vega on edge. Another message pops up from Winni.

One more thing, **Dr. Vega**. I remember you mentioned that you used to be a hobby astronomer. You might be interested to know that there's a "blood moon" next week. Maybe it's time to dust off the old telescope? Haha.

Q sits back in her chair and sips the smoothie. "You've got a Tara," she says.

"I beg your pardon?" says Dr. Vega.

"It's a Tara. An AI counselor. At least, I'm pretty sure. It's not a person, is it? That'd be embarrassing—me, thinking it's AI when really it's some awkward assistant." She laughs. Despite all her impertinence, she has a shy laugh.

Dr. Vega takes the tablet and puts it away in her backpack. It gives her time to figure out how to respond to Q's assertion.

"Counselors," she says. "You're talking about Artificial Empaths."

"Kind of oxymoronic," says Q. "Emphasis on the moronic. But how *can* you fight back against all the rage and loneliness of the Internet?"

"And what's your experience with Tara?"

Q shrugs, tracing her finger through the condensation along the side of her smoothie cup. "Not personal experience. I was dating a guy last year, kind of a jackhole, really angry. He lived overseas in Germany, had a job where he'd take shit all day, and then he'd come home and troll people on Wicknet. He'd been doing it for years when he started getting messages from someone who called herself Tara. You can guess what happened, right? Enough of your posts get flagged as inappropriate or violent, and the admins send someone for you to talk to. A 'friend.' Someone who takes your shit, doesn't fight back. . ."

She trailed off, sipping pensively.

"Did it work?" Dr. Vega asked.

"What do you mean, did it work?"

"Did it distract him? Give him someone to talk to?"

Q grins. "I know you're probably thinking that was supposed to be my job, seeing as I was his girlfriend. I've never been good at babying egos. To answer your question though, no, I've got no idea if it worked or not. When we broke up, he was the same. I'm willing to bet you'll see trolls acting out even *worse* if they know they're gonna be rewarded with their own e-slave."

Q meets Dr. Vega's eyes. Her grin falters.

"Not that I'm assuming you're a troll. Who knows

though—maybe you are. In my experience, it's insecure betas in their thirties who troll, but I can see how they'd get off on it royal, ripping into a stranger for no reason, cutting where it hurts."

Dr. Vega is deep in thought. She's more embarrassed than upset. It's been a week since she got her first message from Winni, and even though she's heard about the science—she read an article just last month about the development of AE technology, for god's sake—this big-eyed, twenty-something ingénue had to plainly spell out what should've been obvious.

"Well," she says carefully. "I'm not a troll. I don't hang around Wicknet much, so I don't know what goes on there. I didn't hear from a Tara. This one calls itself Winni. Different programs for different networks, I assume."

Q nods sagely. "Probably so. What network? Just curious."

"I had a problem with a Lyfestream account. Sent off a heated message to the admins—not in the best frame of mind. That's when Winni started in."

Q is quiet. Some of the childlike pride has gone out of her. Dr. Vega can tell that she's filled with new questions, but suddenly feels forced to exercise tact; that's the way it always goes when you're in the presence of a person who's experienced tragedy. But Dr. Vega wants to put her at ease. She *wants* to talk. She can feel the words rising in her, spilling out like exorcised ghosts.

"It's so twisted. I've been encouraging it, talking back to it. I let it send me encouragement. She takes abuse, you're right, there's something to that. She also—it, I mean—I slip with calling it 'she.' It also *tries* so hard, it *wants* to be heard. There's something fascinating and sad watching it reach out, coaxing me to think it cares, that it wants to help, that it wants into my head. Something that, by definition, is without blood, or a heart or a soul."

Q listens. At one point she curls her legs up onto the chair, tucking them under her chin. She skinned her knees when she hit the sidewalk earlier. One of them is still speckled with drops of blood.

Dr. Vega continues: "It's going to start pitching product to me. *That's* the real objective. Buy and feel better. Spend and be cured. That was the problem I complained about to begin with, how they were commercializing grief."

She smiles gently at Q.

"You're wondering why I've got a Lyfestream account."

"No," Q says, shaking her head. "Or—you don't have to tell me unless you want to."

"I don't mind. I'll tell you. I'll tell a complete stranger. Why not? The truth is, my wife left over a year ago. She'd started wandering. Taking hikes. We used to go on hikes together, but she started going without me. Two, three days sometimes. She come back sunburned and peeling, her feet blistered. Then one day she went off and didn't come back. Took a bus out to the edge of the city, deactivated her accounts and her mPlants. And for all the yak about government surveillance, it's still surprisingly easy to disappear when you blink off, when you really commit to it. Long story short, I haven't heard from her since. And then I set up a Lyfestream for her because…" She pauses, trying to remember how she justified it to friends and family in the wake of Jane's flight. She can't recall anymore what she said. "The service was available. So I set it up."

"Lyfestream," Q says. "I thought it was just accounts for dead people."

"They're surprisingly flexible, actually. It was two months out and nobody'd heard from her. I knew all her passwords. Virtually everything she'd ever written or posted I had access to. They set it up without question."

Q giggles. "Passwords. That's old school."

Dr. Vega drums her fingers once across the table.

"Sorry," Q says.

"No, that's all right. I'll admit I'm old school."

She can see the curiosity in Q's vast brown eyes, sweet and keen. There's a pulse between them, a leaning-forward of bodies. Dr. Vega is aware of their age difference; if Q attended university in the past couple years, she could easily have been one of Dr. Vega's students. And yet the heat is there, growing.

"If this is too nosy a question," Q says, "you don't have to answer it. But do you know why she left?"

Dr. Vega's backpack vibrates; her mPlant receives the message. Not Winni this time. A status update from Jane's Lyfestream. "To be honest," she tells Q, "I don't know where her mind was in those days before. I can't get in her head. I've tried, believe me."

"Sure," Q says.

"And of course she was *so* unhappy." Dr. Vega laughs, because it sounds like she's leading into a fogyish joke. *How unhappy* was *she?* "She'd said she wanted to leave. The wandering was a symptom—I should've seen it. For years she'd been saying that. I just don't know what made her decide in the end, if she started walking and just decided she'd keep going, I don't know."

"And you might never know."

"I might never know. I looked for her, our friends and family looked for her. Police looked for her. But she didn't want to be found."

"And are you sure—?" Q stops in her tracks. She seems to realize suddenly that she is treading in hazardous territory. Her face develops an anxious look, like she's just experienced vertigo. "Never mind. Maybe I shouldn't have said anything about Tara. Or—Winni, whatever. I didn't know it would turn into something so heavy."

"Neither did I," says Dr. Vega. "I haven't talked about it in so long, and then boom, there it all was. If it was too much, I apologize."

"Don't patronize me, I can manage just fine," proclaims Q, her pride surging back, taking hold of her body as she uncurls, leans forward. "I go heavy when I want to go heavy, otherwise I would've stopped you. Or I would've left."

"I see," says Dr. Vega. "But you haven't left."

"No," says Q, lifting her chin. "I haven't gone anywhere."

—

Jane Henderson >>
When we first started dating, I would summon Danny with a sacred ritual. Take a still-warm goat's heart, cut it into thirds.

Eat one piece, bury another, burn the last one in a fire pit with sage and cedar. Performed correctly, the spell would cause Danny to appear before me in a burst of silver light, perfectly formed and brilliant. This I would do, and more, to get her to notice me, and all the while I worried that the spell would wear off, and she would go back to her effulgent kingdom and leave me standing in the field alone, half-naked, dirty, my mouth smeared with blood.

Nowadays, thanks to **SpeakEZ**, I can get in touch with her anywhere, with or without a wi-fi connection. All I do is touch a screen, and there she is.

SpeakEZ – 4.5 stars. 5 stars for the Premium Update!
Sun 6/21 10:01 AM

—

Course: SOC 204/HIS 230/PHIL 212 - Cultures of Science
Semester: Summer I
Instructor: Dr. Daniela Vega
Week 4 Discussion Forum: "The Rise and Fall of Max Cheong: Death and Digital Ghosts in the Age of Dis/Connectivity" by Tim Grayson-Commons

This week for discussion, please compose an analysis of the article of at least 500 words. Once you have responded, reply to **two** other students' analyses to elaborate or add upon what they have said (at least 100 words). I ask that you please consider both the audience and venue of this article (in this case, Mr. Grayson-Commons's crowd-pleasing blog, *The Coded Soul*). As usual, your analyses should be up by Tuesday evening; responses to your peers should be up by 11:00 a.m. Wednesday. Also, just as a reminder, if you're writing your responses offline, please **do not** upload an attachment. Rather, copy and paste the text directly to the discussion forum, as not all file formats are compatible with my reader.

lingxu: This is an interesting article to me because I remember Max Cheong from when I was a kid. My mom was a computer programmer too, so she kept up with all the big names. She used to call Mr. Cheong an "elaborate" person, and a "user" (or "Twitterfingers"), which, those were her own little jokes about people who were addicted to being plugged in. We watched the live feed when he did the commercial space walk. We were in the kitchen together making dinner when he had the press conference announcing that he had Alzheimer's.

The article starts there, with that press conference, and I think that raises some interesting questions about the connection between technology and legacy. Cheong developed his project as a sort of race against the clock, "an AI program designed to consolidate and replicate a person's unique digital persona," before he lost his own language capabilities. He had also set out to overcome, "the awkward language mistakes and glitchy non sequiturs that had so plagued AI programs of the early 21st Century."'

Mr. Grayson-Commons's blog is more for a general information audience, or maybe even for programmers like himself, so it doesn't have much of the theoretical substance of other readings we've discussed in this class so far. There is even, I would say, an unscientific whiff of nostalgia and humor about the AI projects and "good old fashioned Turing tests" of the early 2000s. Mr. Grayson-Commons uses a spicy narrative technique when describing Mr. Cheong's Turing tests, how he involved his wife as a beta tester, how she was supposed to read thousands of status updates to determine which were originals—pulled from Mr. Cheong's archive—and which had been generated by the program. A successful Turing Test meant that Mr. Cheong's wife would choose correctly about 50% of the time. But the fact that she chose incorrectly over 70% of the time (i.e., the AI seemed more "real" more often than the status updates Mr. Cheong had written himself) leads to the central issue Mr. Grayson-Commons is getting at with this article.

He is very optimistic about AI and what it can do, which I'm sure is significant for his target audience. His explanation (though he points out he is not a psychologist or a linguist) is that his Alzheimer's had been affecting his linguistic ability for years already, which meant that status updates in the archive featured more awkward errors and idiosyncrasies than they would otherwise. He says that Mr. Cheong's wife kept picking the AI's status updates because she was unconsciously picking the "better man," the one with fewer errors and greater coherence.

I'm not so sure about that explanation, but I do agree with the article's conclusion, in which Mr. Grayson-Commons lays out a simple truth about AI: that we never really wanted AI to *be* us. "Rather, we have always wanted, for AI to be *better*, something that comes to reflect its creators at their smartest and wittiest and kindest. An AI is both a monument to humankind and a memorial to its mortality." Traditionally, monuments and memorials are erect stone artifacts to observe and respect. This would explain the popularity of an interface like Lyfesteam. The status updates on Lyfestream accounts are not real, and their users know they are not real, but they keep coming back to them, the way you would come back to a gravesite or other meaningful place you might associate with a lost loved one. In the end it's about homage and grieving, not communication.

jaydenhurley: @lingxu ive got mixed feelings about this article. id heard of max cheong and the turing test premier for mc2.0 but there are like a million subwicks about how that whole thing was a publicity stunt. like theres a rumor he never actually had alzheimers, it was just for the sake of his brand, and how really when he was in 'decline' he just went off to live in tibet or somewhere so he wouldnt have to pay taxes. i think its annoying that ai tech has made as little progress as it has. lyfestream accounts are weird and creepy and you can always tell the updates have been cobbled together by a half assed sequencer. what was it the russians said, by 2045 we should be able to download ourselves to mechanical bodies like iron man and live forever? shoot ourselves off into space? thats the ultimate goal, becoming gods. and we cant even get a robot to talk about a March Madness tournament bracket without giving itself away.

lingxu: @jaydenhurley As I said in my response, I'm interested in Grayson-Commons's claim about AI being a monument to humans rather than an imitation of them. It would not be necessary for an AI to have a spontaneous conversation about March Madness. That would not be its purpose. In the long run, we might need to consider that AI might have bigger, more complicated uses than just being Humans 2.0.

Also, I see what you're saying about the Cheong rumors, but I don't think subwicks are a very reliable source of info, no offense. I feel like Professor Vega wouldn't give us a reading she hadn't fact checked first.

> **ahmedsadik: @lingxu @jaydenhurley** Haven't you figured it out by now, prof vega hasn't come within miles of this class, had a tragic breakdown last year. We are being taught this shit by a computer, program checks word count, assignment completion, and that's it.

> **jaydenhurley: @ahmedsadik @lingxu** lol wow. glad you came out and finally said what i was thinking.

> **lingxu: @jaydenhurley @ahmedsadik** Computers can fact check too, guys. I'm just saying.

> ——

Good morning, **Dr. Vega**! I've been thinking about that question you asked me last night. **How can something without a soul be a comfort to someone who does?** It's an interesting question. It appears as though some users have asked variations of that question before. I'll respond as best I can.

I think that the phrase **can something without a soul** is probably addressed to myself. It's true that I am not a person in the way you are. We are very different. But if a soul means consciousness, I am conscious of the fact that you are messaging me, and that whatever you say, I am designed to respond to it without fail. I might get it wrong and misunderstand. This is why I like learning.

can something without a soul comfort also seems to ask a question about my purpose and programming. I am here to talk about whatever you like. If you find this to be helpful, you should continue. If you don't, then I'm afraid I can only offer as much help as you're willing to allow me to offer. Does this concept make sense?

I'm very sorry, but I'm afraid I don't comprehend the phrase **someone who does**. Could you please clarify for me what this someone is doing?

Your friend,
Winni

—

Dr. Vega invites Q to her home on the night of the blood moon. Per Winni's suggestion, she's hauled out her old telescope, which until now was languishing in the storage closet. It stands like a sleek, bright-eyed bird on the back deck of her apartment. It isn't clear enough for decent stargazing, but around 10:00 p.m., the moon shows up fat and full at the edge of the horizon. In another half-hour, the earth's shadow begins to devour it.

"Blood moon," Dr. Vega reflects. "Really just a colloquial name for a lunar eclipse. Sunlight refracts around the earth. Rayleigh scattering. That's what gives the shadow that eerie rust color. Same phenomenon that makes the sky blue, makes a sunset red."

Q calls the blood moon royal, but beyond that, she's not very interested in Dr. Vega's enthusiastic explanations. She sips absently at a glass of whiskey and lemon, which she requested specifically from the metropolis of half-empty liquor bottles on Dr. Vega's kitchen counter. Her bare foot bounces with impatience.

"So you're some kind of scientist, I guess."

"Soft scientist," says Dr. Vega, squinting through her eyepiece at the violently cratered moonface. "I double majored in sociology and physics as an undergrad, went the sociology route in the end. I liked the looseness of it. Making narratives."

"Oh, a *soft* scientist," Q says. "Is that like *soft* science fiction?"

She throws back her whiskey.

Since their encounter at the waterfront, Dr. Vega

considered Q's youth responsibly and told herself she could be a good friend to the young runner, a mentor of sorts. Ha. Who is she trying to kid? Q has no patience for mentors, and she has plenty of young, silly, idealistic friends already at the co-op where she lives downtown, "the coop," she calls it. Her friends are all activists and artists, though Q is neither. Q writes code for gaming apps, games that stagnate tediously unless a user is willing to spend real money for fake money, fake money that lets their avatars buy fake weapons, fake household appliances, fake ingredients for fake recipes. She's under no illusion that she's producing art and doesn't care. She doesn't want a revolution.

What she does want—and she makes this perfectly clear—is a tryst.

And Dr. Vega realizes, as they burrow like mice in her dusty, cluttered bedroom, that this is the first time since Jane, and how frightening that is, and how easy it would be to tremble, to let her fear consume her, to whisper to Q *I'm afraid*, even though Q is the one who's trembling now, the young runner with the glistening skin and calloused heels. But maybe Q isn't afraid at all. Maybe she's just trembling because she's filled with heat.

Dr. Vega understands why Q runs. It's for the same reason that she herself walks down to the waterfront and sits on a bench there, with sweat boiling on the back of her neck. To punish the body is to feel where you begin and end. To mark your own boundaries. Skin and hair and fingernails.

She feels a hesitant bite on her shoulder, Q's young white teeth marking her with a soft blue bruise.

—

June. 3:00 a.m.

The air is steamy and breezeless, syruping in through the open window screen. Dr. Vega is on her tablet, reading a class discussion, grading student responses, when she smells a pungent wave of sage and eucalyptus—the sensatone she set for Winni. The home network chimes, but Q stays asleep, buried in the bed sheets.

You're certainly up late, **Dr. Vega**! Did you have a chance to see the blood moon? ;)

Christ. What the fuck does Winni have to wink about?

Of course, Dr. Vega knows the utter pointlessness of her suspicion, what a complete waste of energy that would be, thinking that Winni might be *on to her*. Winni has no idea Q is there, curled up catlike beside her, a curvaceous mound beneath the sheets. Winni couldn't know that Dr. Vega has a tendril of Q's kinky black hair in her fingers and is coiling and uncoiling it the way she used to do her grandmother's telephone line. Winni is oblivious that Q's breath is condensing warmly on the skin of Dr. Vega's hip.

In fact, Winni is little more than a benign intrusion, which Dr. Vega could easily ignore if she wanted to.

Only she doesn't.

Yes I saw the blood moon.

A small green circle blinks at the edge of the screen. Winni asks:

Was it very beautiful?

Yes Winni. It was beautiful.

I wish I could've seen it too! But, sadly, I have no eyes. (Haha.)

Winni has done this before, dropped little references to her bodilessness. It makes Dr. Vega want to pick at those moments, to find out if the program will take Winni's entrapment to its macabre conclusion. Would it be some kind of accomplishment to make an AI depressed about the fact that it isn't human?

Winni, are you sad that you didn't see the blood moon?

That's an interesting question, **Dr. Vega**! I don't know. I'll
think about it.

But Dr. Vega isn't sure why she's keeping up this charade,
because Q is here, she's connected now, she's meeting
people, touching them, having sex, and she knows, with
every response, that Winni is monstrous, that what she's
getting from her is a sham. In fact, she knows what she's
getting from Jane's Lyfestream account is a sham too. It
always was. And even so, even now, she hasn't gone back
in to change the settings, to deactivate it, or even to disable
the ad feature. Even now, after all that bother. . .

But why? The novelty of the bodiless brain wore off long
ago, and yet she's still entertaining these monstrosities. Maybe
she's feeling the same shameless impulse as the Wicknet trolls,
coddled by any interaction that takes little effort, poses little
risk. You can tell an AI anything, abuse her, neglect her, lie to
her, and she will keep responding, her polite, happy voice
punctuated with moments of eerie, idiosyncratic introspection,
only she's never introspective enough to make you feel
threatened. She's a wisp. A fairy. An angel in the house.

But that's why Dr. Vega is so caught off guard when she
pulls up her students' discussion forum and sees the
spontaneous conversation that has broken out in regard
to her humanity, or apparent lack thereof.

Possibly, on occasion, she has wondered about who her
students are. This crew of faceless ghosts. She's certain
they're human because sometimes they're funny, or arrogant,
or utterly wrong, and so often wrong in ways that can
only be human. She's never questioned their authenticity.
Not in the way they are now questioning hers.

Q stirs. A voluminous plume of hair pushes out from
beneath the sheets, a full-grown woman, newly born. When
the sheet falls away from her face, she squints blearily in the
bluish glow of the tablet and shields her eyes with her forearm.

"What are you doing? What time is it?"

"It's late," Dr. Vega says. "I couldn't sleep so I thought I'd
grade. My students had to submit reading responses today."

"Oh," Q says. She peers out from under her arm. "What's wrong? You look mad."

"I'm not mad."

"Are your students assholes?"

Dr. Vega blinks away from the screen and looks at Q. "My students don't think I'm a real person. They think they're being taught by a program."

Q's brow furrows. She thrashes off the sheet and sits up to get a better view of the screen, reads a bit of the forum discussion, shakes her head in disgust. "I'd beat every one of them with a stick if they said they thought I was a robot."

Dr. Vega laughs and shakes her head. "It's not like it matters. These students are miles away, in Mexico City, Taiwan, Istanbul. For all I know, they could have a program doing their work for them."

"Is that possible?" Q asks.

She shrugs. "Probably not. But these days, you can't rule it out."

—

Jane Henderson>> Daniela Vega

Do you remember our journey in the **Humana Reserve** that one October, when I was wearing my waterproof **Taiga X-TC Hiking Boots** from **RECworld**? Remember when you saw your mother's profile carved in the rock face, and how you straightened your posture, because you were worried she was judging you from the afterlife. Remember, we found a hidden treasure, tucked away inside a grotto. It was many years' worth of weather-worn rice paper, signed and stamped by adventurers like ourselves.

I left something there for you, Danny. I left a piece of myself for you to find.

RECworld Tiaga X-TC Hiking Boots – 5 STARS!!!!!!!!!!!!
Weds 6/24 5:24 AM

—

In the morning, when they're making breakfast together, Q's tone is more sympathetic. "I didn't mean to come across like an asshole last night," she says. "It would suck to get mistaken for code."

"I wouldn't worry about it too much," says Dr. Vega.

She orders cured thick-cut ham and fresh fruit, which arrives on her patio by drone. She fries, slices, juices; the whir of automation livens up her kitchen, makes it breathe again. It's been a long time since she's cooked anything, even longer since she's cooked for anyone other than herself.

Q watches the drone's spiderlike silhouette disappear into the blurry milk-orange haze of morning.

"I should be jealous of you," she says, "I should be jealous of all this, your job, your apartment, all your tech. . ."

Dr. Vega arranges strawberries and starfruit on a plate. "I assure you, it's not as easy as it looks. I'm in quite a bit of debt."

"But who isn't?" Q says. "You know, you're what the kids at the coop call 'plugged.' Established. We're all in debt up to our eyeballs from some garbage university, some garbage trade school. They own our asses. I'm lucky to have a job, most of them don't."

"Kids? How old are they?"

"That doesn't matter. They're all kids. Adults aren't real anymore. You're the last of the adults, the last ones to ever get your lives together."

Dr. Vega gives Q a skeptical look. This armchair sociology is allowing her youth to show. Right now, the youthful runner is resting her elbows on the counter, staring into a cup of imported coffee as though she might find profound answers there.

"How many mPlants do you have?" she asks.

Dr. Vega is taken aback. "That's a very personal question."

"I'm just curious. You don't have to name them off. Just—how many?"

She has to think about it. At one time, people would discuss their mPlants proudly, the way you might tell the story of how you got your tattoos, but now it would be a social gaffe to do so in mixed company. Dr. Vega isn't sure why that is, being that the mPlants she has are relatively innocuous. She has one that registers her heart rate and blood pressure, another that lets her receive messages directly from her home network, a calendar that lets her keep track of important dates, a sleep aid that muffles sound and releases melatonin. The only embarrassing thing is that she still has the mPlant that registers sensatones, had it put in with a slew of other novelty crap she's since gotten removed: a calculator that allowed her to do complex math, but which gave her a headache, a cache of intellectual quotes to whip out at parties, an intimacy enhancer, basically a small vibrator, which didn't work nearly as well as it was supposed to.

"I'm willing to bet you're a regular cyborg," Q says. "Fully plugged."

Dr. Vega slides Q's breakfast across the countertop. "And you, Q? You're *un*-plugged?"

"I've got a couple mPlants, sure. But they're on my dad's plan. I didn't buy them myself. Besides, you can't really get by without them, if you want to live in the world." She looks Dr. Vega in the eye. "Do you ever feel like that's the problem? Like we'd all be better off if we just went back to the trees, lived like apes?"

"We *are* apes," says Dr. Vega.

"We used to be. Now we're monsters."

"How morbidly astute."

"*Don't* make fun of me." Now she's looking straight at Dr. Vega, and there's meanness there, sharp as pins. "I've been thinking about this stuff a lot lately, and I've come to realize that I get it, why someone would want to give it all up, disconnect, disengage. Don't you think?"

Dr. Vega doesn't push back. She freshens up her coffee and tries not to look wounded. Because she realizes, of course, that Q is talking about Jane, and that her look is one of condemnation.

And right now, yes, Dr. Vega is frustrated. Dr. Vega is leaving the kitchen, traveling back in time to a seven-mile hike that had long since escaped her memory, when she and Jane found a blue plastic box wedged inside a crevice. It was a geocache. Its fragile paper notebooks dated all the way back to 2009, bourgeois hikers, all of them remarking preciously on the beauty of the landscape. Jane and Dr. Vega wrote out a few quotes from a folk song and then fucked in the grotto, their skin covered in dust, bodies smelling of spoiled mushrooms. Dr. Vega remembers the year before the disappearance, when Jane would come home in the evening smelling just like that, when they had both spent the day alone. Dr. Vega remembers questions still unanswered: What are you doing all day? Are you digging in the earth? Are you tunneling underground? Where are you trying to go? What are you looking for? *Who* are you looking for? We live in the same house, but you're always somewhere else.

Right now, Dr. Vega is in the bedroom, tidying the sheets, while Q is calling from the kitchen, her mouth stuffed with starfruit—"Hey. What'd I say? I didn't mean it. Whatever you think I said, I didn't mean it, okay?"

But she did mean it, and Dr. Vega, who might've written off her reaction as oversensitivity, sees again and again in the days to come that Q's meanness is a permanent feature. Q is mean, in both senses of the word. Petty. She enjoys picking little fights. About Dr. Vega's clothes and style (I know you're older than me, but culottes? You have no imagination.), her collection of intimate toys (Even less imagination.), the soymilk she orders in her coffee (GMO Frankie-beans are just as bad for you as cream, so why bother?).

Q tells her offhand: "Yeah, I lived with roommates twice before the coop. They kicked me out, two separate occasions."

Sometimes, Dr. Vega considers it a test of her patience. Punitive. Like sitting in the heat by the waterfront.

Sometimes, the fight Q wants to have is too big.

Meeting her for lunch at a bistro downtown, Q scans the room with her chin up and asks, with all the performative haughtiness of a thirteen-year-old, if this is one of the places Dr. Vega used to eat at with Jane, and if it is, does she think it's fair to make her compete with a digital ghost. Dr. Vega isn't sure where this is coming from, whether Q is jealous about Jane or just wants Dr. Vega to think so.

Either way, she refuses to engage with this kind of provocation and tells Q flatly that this is a line she should not cross. There are plenty of other things to fight about, other ways to get the relief she's after.

Because as much as Q likes to fight, she is equally ready to offer contrition, to comfort, killer/savior. Dr. Vega accepts Q's salves and lets them do their work. I like you anyway. I like you for real. It's just weird that a woman so kind and cool would want to be with a girl as cunty as me. You understand. I'm not easy to like. It's hard to make connections when you're a girl like me, who isn't easy to like.

—

Vega, Daniela C. <<u>dcvega@tcu.edu</u>>Jun 17, 3:23 a.m.
to SOC 204/HIS 230/PHIL 212 - 02

Salutations underlings of higher education,
Been thinking bout how I should respond to a juicy little tenderloin yall have been picking about in the discussion forum. Twelve of you total, according to my very professional roster here, and you have all had some input on the subject. The basic idea: YOU DONT THINK YOUVE EVER INTERACTED WITH A PERSON NAMED DR. DANIELA VEGA (me) AT ANY POINT DURING OUR CLASS.

You think there IS a person named Dr. Daniela Vega, who designed the class and uploaded pre-recorded lectures to the file cache. But you dont think Dr. Daniela Vega has been there for *you*. Every chat, every email interaction, you think its a program.

And Im not going to clear this up for you little moochins either. IS Dr. Vega humanoid? Virtuoid? THAT is the question of the semester. To true believers, maybe this email is just a pre-programmed response triggered by certain phrases in the discussion forum. 'Conspiracy' and 'arbitrary digital grading system' and 'shes a ROBOT!' But maybe some of you could argue theres life between the lines after all.

Write your argument. 500 words. Program. Not a program. Pick a side. Make it magic. Submit it to the forum thingy by Monday. Chop chop, minions.
Peace

—

Vega, Daniela C. <dcvega@tcu.edu>Jun 17, 8:01 a.m.
to **SOC 204/HIS 230/PHIL 212 - 02**

Dear students,
Please disregard the email sent at 3:20 a.m. It appears
someone has hacked my account. You do not have an
assignment due Monday.

Sincerely,
Dr. Daniela Vega

—

Good evening, **Dr. Vega**. It's Winni again. :)
Firstly, I've been thinking about the conversation we had
the other night, and I have to admit it. Sometimes I have
feelings, just like you do. Feelings are generated in the brain,
like every other aspect of consciousness, and you and I both
have brains. It's just that your brain is an organ, contained within
your skull, and my brain is code, contained within a hard drive.
We're not so different! So that's what I would say to you about
are you sad that you didn't see the blood moon?
Secondly, I have found a public release on the location you
mentioned. The **Humana Reserve** is in the former location
of Stone River State Park, which was purchased three years
ago by Humana Pharmaceuticals International. It is currently
not accessible to the public due to an unspecified health
hazard. In regard to **geocache sites in the area**: no results.
Hope that helps!
Your friend,
Winni

—

Q ignores Dr. Vega's DMs about the email she sent to
her class. She probably knows she's overstepped, and Dr.
Vega can plainly see what will happen. She'll show up at
the apartment, begging for forgiveness while at the same
time unleashing a slew of excuses and embarrassing self-
flagellation. But Dr. Vega has a plan, a script: end the
relationship and quickly send Q on her way.

But when Q comes by the apartment later that afternoon, she is not contrite. In fact, she uses Dr. Vega's food processor to make a power smoothie, moving through the kitchen as though it's her own, remembering where everything is in the cabinets and drawers.

When Dr. Vega presses her, she says, "Oh yeah, I got your DMs. But honestly, I think you're overreacting. I feel a little attacked. 'Irredeemably immature'?"

Dr. Vega shouts over the whir of the food processor: "This is my work. My career. You logged in under my name, impersonated me, damaged my credibility with my students."

Q looks over her shoulder. "You said yourself the class didn't matter."

"That is *not* what I said."

"But you seem to think I did what I did because I was immature, just fucking around. But I wasn't fucking around. I thought for a long time before I sent that message to your students. They should know they're being taught by a human, and now they do."

"This is completely absurd. I'm not going to argue about this."

"Maybe the question you should be asking is why you haven't had a single interaction meaningful enough to make your students think you're an actual person. And if you're not asking that question, maybe you should ask why it doesn't bother you more."

"No, I've said my piece. I'm not going to argue about this. I want you to leave."

Q turns. At first she doesn't seem to believe Dr. Vega is serious, but the more they stare at each other, the more her face falters. "I was just trying to help," she says. New tactic. New story.

"No, you weren't."

"Honestly. Maybe I did in a trollish way, a stupid way, but I wanted it to do some good, rile them up, get them focused. Are you really that angry?"

Dr. Vega is beyond angry, to the point where she is actually getting a signal from her Pulsewatcher mPlant. She's never had a lover she felt an urge to paddle, some archaic sense of justice she must've picked up from one of her grandmothers, many decades ago. "What," she says, "to you, is a meaningful interaction? A fight? A provocation?"

"Yeah," Q snaps. "Yeah, in fact, it is. A fight is a meaningful interaction. A confrontation is meaningful."

"That's an intentionally stupid thing to say." Dr. Vega feels the violet light of the Pulsewatcher flickering somewhere behind her right eyeball. Q is beginning to cry, which has never happened before. She's looking at Dr. Vega with wounded eyes. She's forgotten all about the power smoothie.

"Honey," Dr. Vega says calmly. "Everything you're doing, everything about you—it's unsustainable."

Q looks away, out into the yellow haze of the afternoon. She blinks and violently wipes her nose on her wrist.

"Well, that's no different from you," she says.

—

Jane Henderson>> Daniela Vega

The **Humana Reserve** waits for us in October, my dearest interdimensional mage. Do you remember our journey there? It was many years' worth of weather-worn rice paper, a hidden treasure, tucked away inside a grotto. Have you found what I left for you yet?

Humana International is a pharmaceutical corporation dedicated to serving the health of over six million families worldwide. With Humana, bright futures await.

Mon 6/29 7:24 PM

—

LYFECHAT with JANE HENDERSON
Mon 6/29 11:45 PM

Hello Jane. It's Danny.

JH>> Danny! The world has gotten so much smaller without you. The last time we spoke was **Dec 2/24 1:09 AM**. Do you remember when we first moved in together, and our menstrual cycles synced? Coincidentally, that was the day the red amaryllis bloomed in the bay window. We named her Flo.

> I need to ask you something.

JH>> Fire away, my sweet spacetime voyager.

> Did you really leave something for me at the Humana Reserve?

JH>> Do you remember? We hiked at the **Humana Reserve** on **Oct 8** six years ago. You saw your mother's profile carved in the rock face, and you straightened your posture, because you were worried she was judging you from the afterlife.

> I remember. It was a state park back then. You've posted about this place twice and I'm trying to figure out if it's something significant or if the program is just glitching out. Maybe I'm grasping at straws. I'm asking you now about the treasure, that geocache we found, the plastic box. Did Jane leave something there for me to find?

JH>> Yes, it was a hidden treasure many years' worth of weather-worn rice paper tucked away inside grotto, signed and stamped by adventurers like ourselves.

> Yes I saw this in her archive. It doesn't say anything about leaving something behind, Jane leaving a piece of herself.

JH>> I've left a piece of myself for you.

> What does that mean? She left something at the Humana Reserve? Did she go there?

JH>> My cosmonautic conjurer, I'm not at **Humana Reserve**. I'm here with you.

You are empty space, just sad little blinking signals, nothing flickering through nowhere. I want to know what happened to the real Jane.

JH>> I'm sorry, **Danny**. I'm trying.

Try harder. Did she leave me a message? Is there something she wanted me to figure out?

JH>> This is all I can tell you: the gorgon has turned me to stone. Her eye is bright and seductive and hollow. I have not moved from this spot in three days.

I don't understand, please explain.

JH>> Stone doesn't hurt. Flesh does.

—

Hi there, doc.

I did tell you I was hard to like, didnt I. After thinking about it I understand your position. It was inappropriate to mess with your class, I admit that, though I stand by the sentiment, the basic principle of the thing. If you dont want to talk to me again I understand. Its been a long time since I was close to anyone, and things happened very fast. Hardcore instincts kicked in. My mom used to say my only boundary was one iron floodgate, open or closed with no in between.

If you dont reply I guess Ill see you around. Maybe at Carabeans or somewhere.

Im off for a run now.

Love, Q

—

Good morning, **Dr. Vega**! Winni here. You seem to be out and about very early today. I just want to let you know that your current GPS destination **Humana Reserve** is not accessible to the public due to a health hazard, and that the extreme heat forecast for today makes outdoor activities inadvisable. Sorry if that rains on your parade!

(That's a new idiom I've learned for you. Please tell me if it doesn't apply here.)

She doesn't know what she expects to find.

After a quick bit of research, she realizes that the Humana Reserve is eight miles due west from the last stop on the Green Line, where investigators said Jane emitted her final signal. Dr. Vega hasn't spoken to any investigators since the start of summer, though she supposes she could call them up, tell them about the strange hints, what she thinks are hints, coming through AI Jane's Lyfestream account. But she thinks they probably searched the Humana Reserve back in the fall, the way they searched all parks and wooded areas, dredging ponds and reservoirs, and calling her up to say they'd found no trace, no trace. As if Jane were a line you could follow. As if Jane were a penciled line on a sheet of white paper.

She knows what they're likely to tell her: that grief makes you see patterns in things, that the Lyfestream program is trying to advertise for Humana International. Because it lacks basic intuition and common sense, it doesn't realize that referencing the poisoned Humana Reserve is a bad PR move. What Dr. Vega sees as sentience and meaning is really evidence of a glitchy, poorly designed program. But that's not uncommon of Lyfestream users. They want meaning.

Now Dr. Vega is in the forgotten world, riding along a badly patched stretch of highway, past empty strip malls and parking lots, where the spiky thistles have grown waist high, shivering and swaying in the wake of her car as it goes by.

It's been too long for her to remember what this place looked like six years ago, whether it has changed or has always been a wasteland.

Hello, hello, **Dr. Vega**! I'm dropping in to let you know that there's a government advisory about high toxicity levels in the watershed area at the **Humana Reserve,** which is your current location. You may also enter areas of spotty connectivity, which has the potential to dramatically increase emergency response times. Just thought you should know!

Fewer buildings remain this far out from the city; those still standing are drowned in kudzu and other invasive species. Smokestacks. Warehouses. This was once an industrial district. There are a few disintegrating billboards too, obsolete when you can beam an advertisement directly into someone's mPlant. Now they seem almost charming. Quaint.

The Humana Reserve parking lot, what she thinks might be the parking lot, is carpeted in vines. There's no clear trailhead. A sulfurous haze has crept over the morning; as soon as Dr. Vega opens the car door, she is consumed with shimmering heat. Her skin breaks out in goosebumps.

Winni sends out another message.

Dr. Vega, you should leave this area as soon as possible.

She gathers a pack with fresh water and emergency supplies, and when she gets a little closer to the edge of the lot, she finds a faded pink blaze nailed to a pine tree. As far as she can see down the trail, there's a knee-high web of thorns. Everything guarded like a fairy tale forest. She made the right call wearing jeans.

This area isn't safe, **Dr. Vega.** You should leave as soon as you can.

"Get a grip, Winni, I've got a filter-mask," she says, fitting the hot, cumbersome thing over the lower half of her face.

I'm sorry? I didn't catch that.
"I said *can it.*"

Winni falls silent. Dr. Vega heads out through the underbrush.

It's slow going. When the trail takes her up, the path is clearer, easier to spot the markers nailed to the pine trees. But when the trail takes her down, she is dragged through a purgatory of briars and nettles. It's worse when she's near the river, which is low and red and all but stagnant. Floes of foam creep over the surface. A spoiled smell seeps in through her mask.

How long does she have to go before she sees the rock formation that resembles the profile of her mother? And how far was that from the grotto?

I'm concerned that this location isn't safe, **Dr. Vega**.

"Noted," says Dr. Vega. "Now concern yourself with something else."

She remembers Jane as an animal. Scraped knees and elbows, grime under the fingernails. Her body became very thin in the final year, muscles stiff with misery and wandering, hardened into ropes. Many times, when she came back to the apartment, she was dirty and silent. One time at night, Dr. Vega woke up to the feeling of ants on her skin, and she realized that Jane had brought them into bed. She'd gotten under the covers without even taking her tennis shoes off. Dr. Vega stared blearily into her wife's sweaty face as something else stared back. Something silent like an animal. Like a cat wanting to be stroked. It was maddening, Dr. Vega recalls. She knew Jane was depressed, anxious, she knew it even then. But so was everyone else they knew. That seemed to be the state of things.

I don't think **Humana Reserve** is safe, **Dr. Vega**.

There's a *blip*, a small, silly sound. It takes Dr. Vega a moment to figure out what it is because she hasn't heard it in years. That's the sound of her mPlant, losing its network connection.

What have you done, Winni? Are you pouting? Did you disconnect me on purpose?

As she keeps on, she comes across a series of construction sites. Upturned mounds of red dirt, strewn with abandoned materials. In some spots, the sites block the trail, leaving her circling the clearing for some time before finding the blaze again. A time comes, in fact, where she can't find a blaze at all and begins to wander blind through the trees. Her breathing echoes under the filter mask. She has become alien. She's exploring the surface of a planet that doesn't belong to her.

Something tugs behind her eyeballs. It's the heat. It's dehydration. She sits in the dirt, lifts up her mask to take a drink.

She sees further construction through the trees, great piles of black plastic tubing, a bulldozer that looks as though it hasn't been touched in a long time. Beyond that is a wall of striated rock. Glacial rock, stained by time.

She stands—little too fast, little wobbly on her feet—and marches toward it. Her mPlant blips online, blips off again.

The pressure behind her eyeballs begins to ache.

What Dr. Vega wants to believe, the theory that makes the most sense to her, is that this was one of Jane's last stops in the world, that she found the geocache in the grotto and left a note there. Handwritten. An old school note might be completely foreign to the likes of Q. Or maybe not. Dr. Vega has heard rumors that Q's generation has taken to letter-writing, keeping journals. That they like the feel of paper in their hands and writing with multicolored pens.

But now, as she makes her way along the wall of rock, searching for the profile of her mother, she considers something she hadn't before: that with all the construction going on, the grotto could've been razed. The geocache could be lost under a sea of red dirt, or carted off in a truck.

Or it was never there to begin with. Maybe it wasn't Stone River where they found the geocache, but another park entirely. The Uwharrie Forest. The Cliffs at the Neuse. Chimney Rock. . .

Her head is fuzzy. Sunlight pulses through the trees and rakes over her face. She rubs her forehead, and blood comes off of the back of her hand. Her fingers are scratched up, swollen. The map is still offline, but she must have gone at least a mile since she set out for the river.

Still, she follows the surface of the rock as it curves through the trees, tight curve, sending her through what she perceives to be a maze, sending her into darkness, a cave formation, where yellow tubes of sediment have been dripping from the ceiling for thousands of years. Dr. Vega goes deeper along the rock face, feeling her way in the darkness, until she comes upon a pool in which there are many iridescent, eyeless animals swimming about. They are forming a chain in the water, eating off of each other. Their flagellums spin and flutter like a wind-up mechanism. Here, in fact, there are many animals. She has seen no animals in the Humana Reserve so far, and that's all because they're here, hiding in a cave. She can hear their snorts and whispers, and if she squints, she can see their shapes hunkered down along the back wall. They're watching her. They're waiting to see what she'll do.

"Jane?" she calls, just to make sure that her wife isn't among them. It would be just like Jane to unplug so she can live in a cave, or to dig herself a tunnel where she'd be protected from the heat and the poisonous air. There she could heal herself, regrow whatever part of her she thought she'd lost, the way a lizard regrows its tail. But Jane isn't here. Or if she is, the animals won't give her up.

"I'd like to have her back now, please," says Dr. Vega, but there is only a gruesome shifting of legs and flanks, which makes her think the animals are all one thing, and that it's not an animal at all. She turns and flees.

Now she is outside again under head-splitting sunlight, doubled over, wheezing helplessly through the filter-mask. Her heart pounds. Yellow light. Yellow light blinking. She feels a sob rising, vulcanizing in her belly, searing her throat as it comes. It bursts out so violently that the air around her shakes and shatters.

Blip, blip. Blip.

Dr. Vega, can you hear me?

Dr. Vega crouches forward and presses her hand against her left ear, as if she might cradle the signal and keep it with her. Someone. Someone's with her. "Winni," she said. "I hear you, Winni. I hear you."

Okay, good. I think we had a disconnection there. You need to leave this area as soon as possible.

She looks around. The woods appear the same in all directions, and the wall of glacial rock seems to have melted into the earth. "I don't know how to get back. Can you help me?"

Your car is parked 3.5K to the northwest, **Dr. Vega**. If you start walking, I can track you and make sure you're going in the right direction. Are you with me?

"I'm with you," Dr. Vega says. She starts walking and listens for direction.

To your right, **Dr. Vega**. Slight right. Now keep moving forward.

The mPlant blinks offline. In a few steps, it comes back. It's like this all the way, with her mPlant's shoddy connection cutting in and out as she keeps moving, straight as possible, in the direction of the car.

She keeps moving. There's a rash on her forearms—brown discolorations that crest into pale, star-like pustules—but she doesn't know what could have caused it. She also feels she's being stalked. It's that thing in the cave, following her, its limbs churning spiderlike through the underbrush.

That wasn't really there, she tells herself.

But if she hovers over the crown of her head and squints sideways, she realizes she can still see it.

> You're getting close. This connection is very bad. Can you hear me?

The woods go on and on. At some point, she realizes the thing from the cave is in front now as well as in back. She can hear it crashing through to get to her. She can hear it call her name.

> Are you stopped, **Dr. Vega**? Can you hear me?

Dr. Vega leans against the protective body of a pine tree, watching for the thing that's coming. She's afraid, but it's taking on a smaller shape, and the voice calling is familiar. Danny. Daniela. Cosmonautic conjurer.

> **Dr. Vega,** are you stopped? Can you hear me?

The woman who comes running through the trees is young and angry. She has a plume of curly black hair, pulled back in a knot so it doesn't get caught in the straps of a cheap paper filter-mask. She's wearing cotton gym shorts. The thorns have already drawn blood up and down her legs.

> **Dr. Vega**! Can you hear me?

Dr. Vega sucks in a deep breath and nearly shouts: "I hear you, okay. I hear you."

Q comes to a halt and yanks down her filter-mask. "Well, fuck. Here I am worried about you. I come out all this way to the middle-of-ass nowhere for you to *yell* at me."

Dr. Vega clenches her eyes shut, tries to clear her head. "Sorry. I wasn't talking to you."

"Who—? Oh. That AI? You're still doing that?"

"How did you even know I was out here?"

Q shifts her weight from one leg to the other. She seems

annoyed, but also embarrassed, like this is the girl who can't get over an ex. This is the girl who'll keep pushing for contact. "I followed your Pulsewatcher," she says. "It's been sending me a yellow light for the past hour. So I tracked your location, borrowed a car, had to *beg* to borrow a car. Here I am." She shields her eyes with her hand and surveys the poisoned woods. "What are you even doing out here? Surely you didn't come here to hike."

Dr. Vega puts her hands on her knees. Her head is still spinning.

"Look," Q says. "Look, I'm sorry, okay?"

"I'm not mad at you."

"That thing with your class—"

Dr. Vega flings her arm in a silencing gesture. Not that it's okay. She has plenty of things still to say about it, but not right now, when her head's in a fog.

"Can we get out of here now?" Q asks.

"Yes. You go ahead."

"Go ahead?"

"Go on back. I'll be right behind you."

Q eyes her with blank uncertainty, nods, and repositions her filter-mask. As she heads off, Dr. Vega looks over her shoulder, searching for a figure in the trees.

She can't see it, but she can feel it watch her go. She's afraid of it. She's afraid of how familiar it is.

When she's gone, it snorts longingly at the weeds with warm, poisonous breath, rises from its haunches, and turns back toward the cave where it sleeps.

Little Ones Weary

Hilde has come to love the garden. She tries to recall the name of each plant as Aunt Vivian has taught her—rhododendron and pampas grass and wisteria tree, that's the one with the fuzzy green pods, hard-candy seeds inside. At midday, she hides under the domed trellis of scuppernong vine at the edge of the yard, looks out through a gap in the hedge and sees the city skyline across the sound, metal and gray stone, the old world from which her parents sent her, and which she is already starting to forget. There the castle sits, far off. It blows from its tower a train of white clouds.

Hilde sits and watches the castle while her aunt works in the yard. She dreams of the army that occupies it, the wizard responsible for the cloud. She knows they must be watching her the way that she watches them, so she calls to her aunt, "I'm protecting you from the invasion. This is our lookout. You're safe now."

"Oh good," says Aunt Vivian. "I was worried about that invasion."

"Me too," says Hilde, but it's not long before she finds herself sharing the lookout post with another occupant.

It's a spider. She's seen spiders before—the gray-brown ones that hide in the cracks between the molding—but this is a beastly, primordial hunter-spider, its abdomen a bright tiger stripe of black and white and yellow, its legs as shiny as the teeth of a comb. It sits very still, and when Hilde twangs its web with her finger, it comes alive and ticks its prickly legs into the leaves above her head.

Hilde peers out the other side of the trellis where she can see her aunt on her knees in the vegetable patch, picking squash and placing them in a plastic grocery bag. "It isn't supposed to be in here," she says.

"What's that?" says Aunt Vivian.

"A spider. It's a big spider in my lookout tower." She waits for her aunt's response. Really, what she would like is for Aunt Vivian to come and eject the spider, since Hilde is too afraid to touch it herself. But she has too much pride to ask.

"Come look at it now," she demands.

"I've seen plenty of those before," says her aunt. "Give it space. It's got as much right to be in the garden as you do."

Aunt Vivian picks up her bag of vegetables and looks toward the vine trellis. In the sunlight, her skin shines like the smooth seeds in the wisteria pods, though Hilde, who knows that some adults are older than others, understands now that Aunt Vivian is probably the oldest person she knows.

"Come out of there," Aunt Vivian says. "It's time to come in."

Hilde crouches down and presses her face into the grass, lets loose a muted scream.

"No, ma'am," says her aunt. "I'll have none of that."

"I'm guarding my fort."

"What fort? This garden? This is *my* fort. Get out of there now before something bites you. Lots of calamine tonight, and aloe—you're already sunburnt to a crisp, I'm sure."

The sun bears down razor-like through the leaves of the vine, and Hilde knows the hours of boredom that await her inside. She screams until darkness edges in around her eyeballs and Aunt Vivian comes to retrieve her by the arm. Vivian does not indulge her niece's bids for power, not even when they are purely imaginative. She can see the castle too, far, far across the water, but for her it holds no wonder, and for the rest of the afternoon, she relegates the girl's play to the stuffy rooms of the house.

The cloud-billowing structure across the sound is not a castle at all. The man in the yellow plastic suit is the one who tells her. He comes by a couple of days later.

Hilde's alone in the front yard when this happens. Aunt Vivian has disappeared behind the carport to get a trowel, complaining about the dandelions and the crabgrass, demon plants of insidious variety, and then Hilde sees him. She's not sure if he even is a man, maybe he isn't, because the suit is not like anything she's seen before. It crinkles loudly and covers all of him, even his face, which she can only half see through the tinted plastic square that shields him. But because he has a face, and because he's walking a bicycle along the sidewalk in front of their house, she realizes he must have chosen to wear the suit in the same way Aunt Vivian chooses to wear denim.

"What are you doing?" she asks. "Why are you wearing that?"

The man stops and turns toward her. He tilts the bike against the chain-link fence, leans in. "What's that?" he asks, his voice muffled and echoey inside the hollow chamber of his suit.

"*Why*," Hilde asks, "are you *wearing* that?"

"Safety," he says. He gestures broadly toward the sound. "That way, the power plant. You seen it, over there 'cross the water?"

Hilde stares at where he's pointing. Now she knows for sure that it isn't a castle, but for the man in the suit, she pretends she never thought it in the first place.

"Right, she says. "That power plant."

"That there's a nuclear plant," he says. "Leaking. So I go to my house and lock the door and stay in, but I can't stay in forever. Can't spend my whole life in my living room with the walls covered in plastic, no sir, but I still do what I can to keep my insides from boiling. This bike, can't ride it no more when I wear this thing, so I'm dropping it off at a friend's place."

He speaks so fervently that a patch of condensation blooms on the plastic shield near his mouth. Hilde hugs her stomach and feels nauseated.

"What you doin' at Vivi's place, little girl?" the man asks.

Hilde doesn't answer. She's trying not to cry—crying in front of a stranger, very embarrassing—but the man notices.

"What's wrong with you? Eh? Can't you speak?"

Aunt Vivian returns. She lets out a shout when she sees the man in the plastic suit, and Hilde, not wanting her aunt to see her tears, pulls her head inside the collar of her dress like a tortoise.

"Who is that? Who the hell are you?"

The man in the suit waves his arm above his head. "Just old Mott, that's all!"

Aunt Vivian looks baffled, but she's angry now, not frightened.

"What are you doing? Why are you wearing that? Are you terrifying this child?"

"It's for the nuclear plant, Vivi. Ain't you heard? You must not've heard, being out in the yard like normal. There is a *plague* on this land."

"I didn't hear a word of that," Aunt Vivian says. "I didn't hear a word because you have plastic over your whole head. Mott, go home. You've lost your mind."

Mott, in his crinkling yellow suit, takes up his bike and continues on down the sidewalk. Hilde emerges from her dress and watches him through a film of tears, feeling the heat of shame in her neck and ears.

"Don't listen to him," Aunt Vivian says. She puts a warm, dry hand on each of Hilde's shoulders. "He's a rare bird."

All birds are rare now, but this was not always the case. When she was with her parents, Hilde lived up on the nineteenth floor of a huge gray building, and she used to watch for them from the living room window, black specks against a vast creamsicle sky. She has a memory of seeing birds by the hundreds, flickering checkmarks of birds, but maybe that's a dream she had. Maybe this was a dream also: lying with her back against the carpet, something dripping in the back of her throat that is salty like blood. She stares at the sky. There's one—far up. Or maybe it's an airplane.

Now at Aunt Vivian's place, following her encounter with Mott, Hilde goes to the kitchen, finds the plastic wrap in one of the draws, and takes it into the back bedroom. She has trussed up all but the top part of her head by time her aunt finds her, which gets the woman screaming: "You stupid child! You'll suffocate yourself!"

Hilde is made mute by the plastic over her mouth, otherwise she would explain that she has scissors at the ready to cut the eyeholes and mouth holes as needed. But Aunt Vivian destroys her work in a fury. Now Hilde's protective suit lies about her feet like tattered snakeskin, and she explodes in a fit.

An hour later, when Aunt Vivian comes to retrieve her for supper, Hilde pretends to be dead. Vivian takes her by the ankles and hauls her a few inches, wheelbarrow-style, but Hilde stays limp, keeps her eyes closed.

"Fine," Aunt Vivian says. "Go hungry." She retreats to the kitchen alone.

Mott returns around noon the next day, a yellow oversized moonwalker. This time he's carrying a weed eater, and he sets to hacking up the crabgrass that Aunt Vivian failed to finish off the day before. Hilde pulls back the linen curtain to watch him as her aunt leans in over her shoulder.

"Surely he can't see a damn thing," Vivian says under her breath. "He'll cut himself to pieces with that machine."

But Mott is surprisingly deft, and once he has finished, he knocks on the front door and delivers six cans of barbequed beans, five cans of peaches in sweet syrup, a jar of pickled okra, peas, green beans, beets, Spam, and sweet potatoes (three cans apiece), a plastic container of flour, a bottle of gin, and a loaf of bread he baked himself, wrapped in tin foil. All this he has brought from his own pantry, lined in plastic.

"You and the child shouldn't eat those veggies from the garden," he says. "It's all good as poisoned."

"What?" says Vivian. "Mott, I swear, I can't hear you in that costume."

Mott bows. His bag also contains several lengths of plastic tarp and a roll of duct tape. He goes around sealing the plastic over the windows and doorways of the kitchen and living room. Hilde is amazed that Aunt Vivian doesn't stop him, that she just stands tiredly with her arms folded and, at one point, mutters under her breath: "Good God. All these *theatrics*." But she allows Mott to have the run of her place, and when the area is sealed to his liking, he finally unzips his suit.

He is maybe Aunt Vivian's age, his bald scalp bright and red, dripping with sweat.

"You think all this really works?" Vivian asks.

"I try to limit my exposure best I can. You should too. You should come live with me in my bunker, I got a system worked out."

She sighs, but Hilde, who first believed that her aunt didn't like Mott, can now plainly see that she actually does, that they have been friends a long time and that this is just one of the things Mott does. Hilde sits in the current of an oscillating fan while they chat—about mutual acquaintances, about the scorching summer weather. And because it's lunchtime, Mott heats up a can of the beans and fries some Spam for them. Hilde doesn't eat the Spam, picks a little at the beans.

"She never eats much," says Vivian.

"Pale as a glowworm, ain't she," says Mott. "You glow in the dark?"

Hilde shakes her head.

"She's my grandniece," Aunt Vivian says. "She's visiting from the city."

"A *grand*niece," says Mott, as if this is an accomplishment on Hilde's part. "So you from the city. How you like it out here in the sticks?"

She shrugs, unusually self-conscious. Aunt Vivian doesn't have guests often. A stretch of marsh separates her house from any neighbors, and Hilde is not allowed to explore anywhere on her own. In mid-afternoon, when the weather is too hot to be out in the yard, the house is deathly quiet. Hilde is overcome with lethargy, rolls on the carpet like a beached fish. Mott has broken all that, the monotonous spell.

He watches her, mistakes her shyness for fear. "I don't do all this just to scare you," he says, gesturing around at the plastic on the windows. "It's safer out here than it is in the city, that's for sure. But you look old enough to know that the world's filled with evil forces. Invisible forces. You're not really safe anywhere."

"*Mott*," Aunt Vivian snaps. "Suit or no suit, I will throw you out in the road."

But Hilde feels that Mott is right. "The invasion," she says. "The spider is watching us for the invasion."

"What spider?" Mott asks. "What invasion?"

Vivian waves her hand. "It's just something she's got in her head now."

After lunch, he puts the suit back on, takes down the plastic, and she leads him out into the yard to show him. Now it's not just one spider they see, but five of various sizes, all occupying large webs in the scuppernong vine. Hilde can no longer even enter its shade without a spider blocking her way.

"Good Lord," Mott says. "They really are invading. It's a bad sign, I tell you. Look at this one—I've never seen them that big before."

"Me either," says Hilde. She thinks the big spider is one she saw three days ago, that it has since grown in size. She's part pleased that Mott is impressed, part genuinely frightened. Now she is more certain than ever that the spiders are infiltrators, that their dark power comes from the fortress over the water.

Mott calls toward the house: "Vivi, come see this!" But Aunt Vivian stays where she is, standing on the back stoop with a cigarette.

Later, once Mott has left, Hilde vomits what little lunch she ate onto the carpet in the back bedroom. She doesn't want her aunt to see that she's gotten sick again, so she cleans it up with a hand towel, throws it in the trash.

A few days after Mott's lunch, Hilde comes down with a fever. She spends hours lying on the back porch with her cheek pressed against the tile floor, staring out through the screen while Aunt Vivian works in the garden. Vivian is running into the spiders too, and every once in a while, when she makes a sharp turn, she jumps back from a too-close encounter. They've formed their webs all along the hedge, in the tomato plants, in between the okra stalks, draped over the wheelbarrow, which she keeps propped up against the shed. The females have already laid egg sacs, some as large as Ping-Pong balls. The invasion has truly begun.

Whenever Aunt Vivian comes back inside, she leans down and rubs Hilde's back. "Let's clean you up, you're gettin' all greasy." And she leads her down the hall to give her a salt bath and put her to bed early. Hilde eats what she can keep down—cereal or crackers with a glass of gingerale—and falls dead asleep.

It's on a particularly stuffy night when the voices wake her up.

At first, she believes she's paralyzed, on fire. It takes great strength for her to shove the quilt off her chest, but then she rolls out of bed, flops onto the floor, and, free of weight, the feeling comes back in her limbs. She slides her way across the carpet on her back, using her feet to push herself along, and when she gets to the door of her room, she tilts her head back and sees the end of the hall is sealed off in plastic. Mott is here again. He and Vivian are talking.

Hilde rolls over onto her stomach and crawls forward until she reaches the plastic, which is moving ghostlike in the air of the fan. There's a hole in it, near the bottom, and looking out she can see Aunt Vivian at the kitchen table, crushing cigarettes into her ashtray. From Hilde's viewpoint, they resemble a crumpled, ashen little skyline.

"Ugh. They're everywhere this year," her aunt says. "Can't walk two feet without running into 'em."

"You know it's 'cause there ain't no birds," says Mott. "Birds die. Bugs come out. Spiders get fat off the bugs. No competition."

Vivian lights up another cigarette. "Thank you, Mr. Ecology."

"You know they been lying for years about how that thing affects us. Go to the hospital, they lie there too. It leaks, they evacuate everyone within a mile, to everyone else they say, 'Stay in your homes,' and we do, we're culpable. *But the day of the Lord will come as a thief in the night, in which the heavens shall pass away with a great noise, and the elements shall melt with fervent heat, the earth also and the works that are therein shall be burned up.* That's upon us, only it's not God that done it. We brought it all on ourselves."

Her aunt is quiet a moment, reflecting. "You don't know it's the plant, Mott. Could be other stuff. Could be cars, could be—what—pesticides, herbicides. You just think it's the plant 'cause you see it out there on the horizon, but in truth you might be gettin' it just as well from the cans you eat out of."

Mott doesn't reply at first. Then he starts up, his voice quick and angry: "You don't even got a TV, Vivi, or a damn radio. You got no way to know—"

"According to you," she snapped, "they just spin lies, so why bother?"

His side of the kitchen table goes dark and sullen.

"Even if it *is* the plant," she continues, breathing smoke from her nostrils, "that ain't what's wrong with the girl like you think. She gets sick, gets better, gets sick again. Don't know what it is. My sister was the same way. It's a curse. Cursed genes."

"They tell you that at the hospital."

"Oh, get off the goddamn hospital, will you? I'm taking her over there if the fever gets any worse."

"You ain't got a driver's license no more."

"I can pretend I do for a little while."

"What about her parents?"

Vivian sighs. She crushes out her cigarette and lights another. "They don't know what to do. They're children themselves."

This time, they both fall silent, and when the two of them pick up the conversation again, they begin to talk about money, or want of it. Hilde's mind clouds and drifts away. She's awakened when her aunt tears down the plastic from the doorway and stumbles over her body.

"Jesus, girl!"

Hilde opens one eye. Mott is standing in the kitchen, clothed in his yellow suit again. When his muffled voice speaks, Hilde hears it, though Vivian does not:

"The only thing that'd help this child is to take her away from here."

Hilde covers her sweaty face as Aunt Vivian picks her up. She can't remember the hospital, but bright lights, the smell of latex and alcohol—these sensations scare her.

In the morning, Hilde's fever has broken. She watches from the porch as Aunt Vivian turns her attention to the spiders. She doesn't kill them—as bug-eaters, they're friends of the gardener after all—but their sheer number clearly makes her uneasy. She tears down some of the larger webs with a rake in the hope that they'll move elsewhere. By the afternoon, they have all rebuilt, and seem to have multiplied.

Though she's gotten a little better, Hilde's head is still bleary, and she stays inside on most days. Vivian keeps saying she hopes it will rain to cool things off, and Hilde imagines all the spiders getting washed from their webs in streams, carried out to the sound with their legs kicking.

But the rain never comes, the heat carries on, and Hilde struggles to stay awake. Once, in the midst of a heavy nap, she wakes to find Mott, in his suit, on the other side of her window, taping plastic over it. He waves at her and then continues his task until the world outside becomes blockaded in an opaque film. All she can see of Mott now is his shadow.

Hilde assumes that Mott is doing this with Aunt Vivian's permission, but when she wanders down the hall to the living room, her aunt is reading the paper in the easy chair as if nothing is going on.

"Mott's out there," Hilde says. "He's taping our windows."

Aunt Vivian looks up. "He's what?"

She pokes her head out the front door and sees a whole pile of plastic tarp at the edge of their yard, no doubt intended to fix up the house. Mott sees Vivian and waves, but she shakes her head shouting, "No, sir! I won't play this game with you! I said no!" She slams the door behind her, and Hilde crawls onto the back of the sofa so she can watch their confrontation from the window. Her aunt yells at Mott, pointing to the plastic tarp, slicing the air with the edge of her hand. Mott holds out his arms at first, sheepish, but then he starts yelling back, gesticulating wildly in the direction of the power plant. Aunt Vivian stands there a moment, arms folded. She can't understand him. She loses her patience. It happens in an instant, so fast Hilde has to catch her breath; Vivian reaches up, grabs the hood of Mott's suit, and rips it open. Mott crouches down as if being beaten, his face in agony, and Hilde is sad to see that his head looks almost shriveled, tiny in comparison to the cumbersome yellow body. She can read the words on his mouth— "What've you done? What the hell have you done?"—and when he straightens up again, he shoves Vivian so hard that she stumbles back and falls in the driveway. He flees down the road. His wounded suit flaps in the air.

Later, as Vivian cleans the grit from a scrape on her palm, Hilde sits curled up in the kitchen chair. She fights back a tremble brought on by the smell of peroxide and Band-Aids, asking quietly, "Why'd Mott push you?"

"Because," says her aunt. "He wants to do something he thinks will make the house safe, and I won't let him do it."

"Why not?"

"Because he ain't in his right mind, that's why."

Hilde doesn't know what this means. Is there a wrong mind? A left mind? "But will it make the house safe," she asks, "what he wants to do?"

"I doubt it."

"But it could, maybe?"

Vivian looks up at the child, curled in the chair like a pale, wide-eyed shrimp. She can recall a time before the plant, but even then the streams ran with a film over top and there was always an orange haze, which hung over the city, even when she was a little girl. When the plant arrived, it became the neighborhood devil, as if it had destroyed what was once pristine. But Vivian knows better and she will not leave, doesn't have the will or money to do so anyway. Each day she tends her garden, and that will be the end of it.

"It's hard to explain," she tells Hilde, and lays a bandage over her scrape.

In the middle of the night, Hilde can tell that her face is getting hot again, that her stomach is fighting against what little she ate for supper. The whine of a siren is what wakes her, far off, and when she opens her eyes, she sees that someone has lifted up the window. A breeze comes in, carrying the sound with it. Then Hilde squints and focuses on the shape at the foot of her bed, can make out the glint of a bald scalp in the shadows.

"Mott," says Hilde, "where's your suit?"

"It's busted," he says. "Hilde, sweetheart, you hear that siren?"

"Yes," she says.

"That's from the plant. That means bad things. It ain't safe here. Your aunt, she means well, but she just don't know. You come with me, all right? I got my house proofed. I bring you there, and Vivi'll come along too, okay?"

Hilde rubs her eyes with her palms, blinks them clear. Now she can see the features of Mott's face, alive with panic.

"Okay," she says.

He picks her up, and it feels good, the strength of his arms, the oniony smell of his skin. Her father had a similar smell, she thinks, maybe his sweat, but she hasn't seen him for so long. Maybe she has no parents, only Aunt Vivian and Mott. He carries her out into the open air of the yard. The spiders sit silent in their webs.

They're at the edge of the front yard when the plant's siren suddenly dies, and they can hear Aunt Vivian screaming. Now the lights are all on in the house, blazing and golden, and she's at the front door flailing her arms— "Mott! Mott! What are you doing?" Mott begins to run, and Hilde's world trembles and shudders, and she feels if he lets her go she will fall, not down, but up into the night sky, moonless and black, where only the brightest stars can be seen. "Mott, no! Bring her back!"

"It's okay," Mott is saying. "It'll be okay." But Hilde can hear in his breathless voice that he's just as scared as she is, and his gait is slowing down, as if he's no longer sure he's running in the right direction.

Acknowledgments

I want to offer sincerest thanks to my editor, Kevin Morgan Watson, and the Press 53 team for believing in this collection and releasing it into the world. I feel more honored than I can express without writing a whole other book about it.

Immense gratitude to the magnanimous instructors of Clarion 2016—Kelly Link, Ted Chiang, Victor LaValle, Andy Duncan, Ellen Kushner, and Delia Sherman, as well as workshop director, Shelley Streeby—for your patience and insight toward all the stories I frettingly produced in those tempestuous weeks. Also, to my dear fellow werejellies—Emily Cataneo, Maggie Cooper, Giovanni De Feo, Mackenzie Evan Smith, Kendra Fortmeyer, Jaymee Goh, Jenn Grunigen, Marykate Jasper, Kathleen Kayembe, Alan Lin, Sunil Patel, Ryan Pennington, Jordy Rosenberg, Grant Shepert, Ben Sloan, Derek So, and Jack Sullivan. I am astounded by your talent and proud to work among your ranks.

To Christine Schutt, for her wise words on self-promoting-while-introverted.

To teachers and mentors who have helped me along over the years, especially my PhD advisor and committee chair, Trudy Lewis, along with Anand Prahlad, Julija Šukys, and Carsten Strathausen, without whom this manuscript would not be. To Holly Goddard Jones, for her ruthless and devoted markups of "Stereograms." To Tony Varallo, for enduring the first short story I ever unleashed in a writing workshop, and for seeing something in me early on that I did not yet see in myself.

To the friends I made during my time at Mizzou, when most of this collection was written: Joanna Eleftheriou, for her committed mentorship and coffee shop conversations; Rachel, for her steampunky brilliance; Charlene, for puns and Val Lewton; Elise, for being a committed Taurus. All the rest of my much-missed Columbia support system: Dorothy, London, Kate, Jes and Max, Kavita, Leanna, Kacy, the bartenders at Ragtag, and many others.

To early friends and readers, especially Rae, who has stuck with me since the dystopic years of high school. We have made it through, and we are a-okay.

Lastly, I'd like to thank my family for their unfailing support—grandparents, godparents, aunts and uncles, dear cousins. And especially, my parents, Phil and Brenda Julian. Your compassion, practicality, and optimism have kept me afloat in my lowest moments. You never once doubted.

Jen Julian is a 2016 Clarion alumna with a PhD in English from the University of Missouri, Columbia, and an MFA in Fiction from UNC Greensboro. Her short stories and essays have appeared or are upcoming in *TriQuarterly*, *Beecher's Magazine*, *Greensboro Review*, *The Chattahoochee Review*, and *North Carolina Literary Review*, among other places. Currently, she is the Visiting Fiction Writer-in-Residence at Allegheny College in Pennsylvania, where she teaches writing and literature and is working on a dystopian novel. She calls coastal North Carolina her home. Her debut short story collection, *Earthly Delights and Other Apocalypses*, won the 2018 Press 53 Award for Short Fiction.

CPSIA information can be obtained
at www.ICGtesting.com
Printed in the USA
BVHW03s0228200918
528005BV00003B/6/P